THE DEMON'S SHIFTER MATE

Also by Amanda Reid

Enchanted Rock Immortals World Novellas

The Wolf Shifter's Redemption

The Demon's Shifter Mate

The Flannigan Sisters Psychic Mysteries

Finders Keepers

Ghosts, Pies, & Alibis

Murder Most Merry

Fourth and Long

Ghosts, MOs, and a Baking Show

Crash and Burn

Gossip, Ghosts, and Grudges

Seasons Slayings

The Enchanted Rock Immortals World

Releases by Author

Eve Cole

Avian

Fenley Grant

Sorcery, Snakes, and Scorpions: A Love Story

Robin Lynn

Of Magic, Love, and Fangs

Susan Person

Fae Undone

Amanda Reid

The Wolf Shifter's Redemption

The Demon's Shifter Mate

THE DEMON'S SHIFTER MATE

AN ENCHANTED ROCK IMMORTALS NOVELLA

AMANDA REID

Cover Art by Book Cover Insanity, at bookcoverinsanity.com

ISBN: 978-1-951770-04-4

Created with Vellum

THE ENCHANTED ROCK IMMORTALS

Demons and Vampires. Elfs and Fairies. Mages and Witches. Werewolves and Dragons. Psychics and Telekenetics.

These magical beings and more exist, rubbing shoulders in their daily lives with unsuspecting humans. But it doesn't happen without order. Millenia ago, the clans—Sanguis, Fae, Magic, Shifter and Human Paranormal—wisely formed a Council to maintain that order. The end? To ensure the worlds of human and paranormal beings didn't collide and break out into a war that would result in the extermination or subjugation of either.

As human civilization progressed, the first council formed the All Clan Charter at the natural vortex in Great Zimbabwe giving each clan a voice in the administration of affairs both between the clans and with humans. Next, Asia formed its council at Chengtu Vortex. Then European at Warel Chakra Vortex. North America came next at the natural vortex humans called Enchanted Rock in what today is known as Texas.

Now, thriving communities of paranormal beings exist in and around the granite outcropping. Humans scrabble over the dome, not suspecting an entire city exists within its confines: The North

American Council and all its departments—Legislative, Administrative, Security, Medical, Vortex Transportation, and Legal, plus restaurants, clan hotels, and shops catering to the paranormal crowds.

Also under that dome? Intrigue, politics, and most importantly, love. These are the stories of The Enchanted Rock Immortals.

CHAPTER 1

Moonlight Lily Foster—Lily to her friends, of whom she counted very few, and 'Chip' to her Hebert Security team—stomped down the corridor of chiseled pink-brown granite. Fae lights lit her way to the clear glass doors marked 'North American Council Security', her destination. The force she used to yank open one of the heavy panels should've ripped it from its hinge, but NAC obviously considered their personnel when they built the stupid thing.

A shame. Paranormal beings could wreak a lot of havoc with little effort. And she really wanted to destroy something right now. Shattering plate glass of this size would've been immensely satisfying.

The NACS office transitioned from the raw rock walls to a sterile finished interior, except for the floor, which had been ground and polished to a high shine.

Chip's combat-booted steps echoed the short distance to the front desk where a woman from the Human Paranormal Clan, by her scent, sat listening to a headset, her forehead resting in the crook of her thumb and index finger. Her coal-black hair had been scraped back into a bun, standing stark against the paleness of her skin. A name plate on the corner of the tall counter ringing the receptionist's desk read 'Talia Johnson'.

"I understand you wish to talk to him, but Deputy Director de Vrys is away at the moment." Pause. She dramatically flopped against her chair's back, arms hanging limp, and stared at the ceiling. "No, I cannot make him answer his phone, sir. When I hear from him, I will give him the message you wish to speak to him."

Great. Simon de Vrys, Chip's point of contact for his assignment, wasn't even here. Irritation bubbled in her blood. What had she done to deserve this? Did her boss, Nathan Hebert, think she pissed in his jambalaya, so he'd decided to volunteer her to Council Security? He hadn't given her a reason, only gave her the order. *Simmer down. The job should only be for a day.*

The young woman behind the desk straightened and ended her call with a stab of her index finger to her earpiece. She muttered to herself as she tugged her black NACS-logoed polo back to rights from her dramatic display. Despite Chip's wolf-shifter enhanced hearing, she couldn't quite make out the other woman's snarled words, other than 'asshole'. That the word came from someone with such delicate features, like the antique porcelain figurines Aunt Hetty collected, sparked unexpected humor.

Talia turned to her with a smile, the welcome diminished by the gritted teeth underneath. "Can I help you?"

Since she'd only ever gained average human woman's height and not that of the usual freakishly tall wolf shifter female, Chip didn't have to bend to prop her elbow on the tall counter. She rested her cheek in her hand. "Sounded pesky. Need me to handle him for you?"

"Ever met someone for the first time and you wanted to buy them a toaster for their bathtub?" Talia quirked a slim black brow with her deadpan delivery.

Chip chuckled. "Yep." She'd always heard working at NAC compared to working with a bunch of constipated, incompetent bureaucrats. If Talia was any indication of the people who worked here, maybe the assignment wouldn't be so bad after all. Only a day, according to Nathan, right? "I'm supposed to see Simon de Vrys, but it seems I missed him. Guess I'll head on back to Morgan City." She pushed off from the desk and started to pivot away.

Talia's eyes grew round. "Wait—are you Chip? *The* Chip Foster?"

The shock lacing her tone didn't surprise Chip. Most assumed by the nickname, the tracker extraordinaire must be a male. Not to mention a female wolf shifter working security, let alone the best nose in the business, shocked many. The wolves of the pack she had belonged to long ago preferred their females in their dens, pregnant and birthing pups by the dozens. Chip suppressed a shudder at how close she'd come to that lifeless existence. "Nope. Everyone knows Chip Foster is a male, so I'll be off."

"No. You *are* Chip." Surety rang in her tone.

Damn it. Talia must be a mind-reader. Chip hastily assembled her mental barriers. Living around wolves, she didn't need to worry about someone barging through her gray matter.

"Yeah," Talia said with a nod of her head and a rueful smile. "I try not to use it too much in the office, though, unless asked. Tends to piss people off." She touched her earpiece. "Sir. Chip Foster's here." An evil glint flashed in her eyes. "Sure. I'll tell *him* you'll be right out." She tapped her finger against the wireless headset again, apparently to end the call.

"You're not very nice."

Talia's slight shoulders shrugged with Chip's chiding as if to say, 'And?'

A smile threatened to erupt, and Chip ruthlessly suppressed it. She used the assumption the name belonged to a male all the time to keep people off balance. And it seemed to suit those who were in the know not to let the unwary in on the joke. Ah, the gallows humor of the security world.

Heavy footsteps sounded in the distance, and for some reason, the rhythm beat ominously, matching Chip's pulse. They tread closer, until a male strode from a hallway behind and to Talia's right.

Chip shook off the silly feeling of foreboding. Especially since merely a man, a Human Paranormal sniffed by Chip's senses, wouldn't cause such a reaction. Strong chin with a slight dimple, sharp wings for cheekbones. Slightly taller than average human males, with wide shoulders, thick biceps, and corded forearms peeking from his short-sleeved NACS polo. Impressive for an HP, since most of the males in other clans didn't even have to work out to manage a ripped body.

Something tugged at her nose. A whiff of...what? She couldn't make it out. Woodsy. A hint of smoke? Interesting cologne. And strangely attractive to her.

She sketched another assessing glance at the handsome specimen, a strange itch in her fingers to run through his thick, dark brown hair. Maybe... She gave herself a mental shake. No. It'd been three years. Anything she needed in that department she could do herself or it could come with a battery. She assumed a position of nonchalance, hip propped against the half-wall of Talia's desk to see what he'd do next.

He scanned the small waiting area. "Where'd he go?"

"Who?" Talia's innocent face gave nothing away. Impressive.

"Chip Foster?" he said with the barest suggestion of exasperation gathering between dark brows.

"I'm Chip Foster." She added a half-cocked brow to the suggestion of a sneer she used when first meeting anyone. Better they know first off not to fuck around with her. That's how she'd earned her nickname. Professionally, she carried a chip on her shoulder the size of Enchanted Rock itself and she'd happily use it to bludgeon anyone who crossed her.

The man's dark brown eyes widened fractionally, but he came

forward and stuck out his hand. "Calum Stavros. Simon was called away unexpectedly and asked me to take care of your arrival." His words carried no hint of emotion, not even a whiff of annoyance and zero hint of a welcoming smile.

She took his hand and its size enveloped her tiny one with warmth, but not the usual crushing-grip bullshit so many males tried to play. Or the crappy, limp-fish one some men believed charming, yet made her upper lip lift in a snarl. But if he was merely Simon's hey-boy, maybe even some admin person, he wouldn't need to play power-games. He must be here to show her the mountains of bureaucratic forms she'd undoubtedly have to fill out to finish whatever super-secret squirrel mission she'd been loaned out to do. Either NACS didn't trust her boss with the information, or Nathan didn't want to tell her.

"If you'll follow me." Without another word, Stavros turned and strode back the way he came, obviously expecting her to follow him. His much longer legs ate up the distance.

She'd follow, but at her own pace. Sometimes she loved playing Chip Foster.

With a conspiratorial smile to Talia, she sedately rounded the desk, only to find the corridor's short expanse empty. A little surprising for an admin person to abandon the specialist they requested, right? Maybe he didn't put himself above little power games.

Hah. She'd grown up with them her entire life. Dominance was the wolf-shifter's national pastime.

Challenge accepted.

She examined the sterile hallway before she entered it. Blank walls with rows of closed brown doors ran down either side, then a dead-end with what appeared to be hallways stretching in either direction. She usually kept the mental lid mostly closed on her scent senses. Otherwise, she'd be overwhelmed by the world around her. She nudged the lid open a fraction more. Ugh. Too much. She pushed back the earthy-metallic scent of the granite permeating the space, the chalky drywall, paint, fae lights with their sprites, traces of elf, shifter, witch, every other scent except for the woodsy-smoke which had taken root in her nose.

No need to shift for this one. Calum Stavros wouldn't be able to hide from her.

Forward, her nose said, and she complied, steps confident down the hallway, but watchful, in full tracking mode. She wouldn't put it past them to test her beyond her tracking specialty. *Bring it.*

She passed the first row of doors to the end of hallway. She turned her nose down the short stretches of passages on either side. Wait. Where did it go? She sniffed in either direction, then took in a bigger breath. Nothing.

Intriguing. She retraced her steps, pausing at each door, eight in total. He hadn't gone in any of the rooms. Back at the T-intersection, she turned right. A couple more steps. Nope.

Several paces the opposite direction determined he hadn't gone this way either.

Chip tamped down the hasty wolf instincts urging her toward frustration. Hasty meant sloppy. Again at the intersection, she sucked in a deep breath and held it while she opened her senses as wide as her human form would allow. She could manage scents easier as a wolf, but she'd have to shed her clothing to shift, and the first day probably wasn't the time for the new girl to get naked. Though her wolf side danced on her paws at the idea she could run free, nudity usually made non-shifters uncomfortable. Or gave them the wrong idea.

She beat back the swamp of essences, funks, and odors until she finally found the one she sought. Still here but masked. Not well enough. She suppressed the fangy smile threatening to erupt. Instead, she closed her eyes, felt for any currents of air. Her shifter-sharpened hearing picked up a rushing vent down the side passage over her left shoulder. She turned her head. But she'd gone down that way and saw nothing.

Trust your nose, girl. It'll never betray you. Aunt Hetty's words floated back to her and it clicked.

If he had cloaked himself somehow... Ah. The smoky aroma. Not cologne.

Demon.

One had murdered Aunty Hetty, earning the clan Chip's eternal suspicion. Clan Sanguis. How he could reek so of the Human Paranormal Clan and so little of what he truly was. Later. Now she had to pass this test. If she'd gone down both hallways and scented nothing, that meant he had to be at the intersection, close to her, maybe only feet away. She used her ability like a scanner, moving back and forth, narrowing on the spare molecules escaping his shroud. She edged closer to a wall. He stood...there.

Her gaze swerved from the exact spot and she moved past him as if still searching. Then she whipped around and kneed what she believed would be the side of his thigh, where a strike to a nerve bundle should bring him to his knees.

A groan indicated she'd connected.

Just not with his thigh.

CHAPTER 2

Not only should he have known Chip Foster was a female, Cal should've known better than to let his little test go on so long. The Priority One investigation demanded his full attention. And he certainly shouldn't have allowed her to discover he could cloak himself as would a full-blooded demon. Especially since his nads now felt like giant throbbing coconuts.

Luckily, he'd managed to hold onto his invisibility, so the intriguingly petite wolf-shifter in front of him wouldn't know how bad she'd gotten him. Right now, as he sucked air carefully through his nose to manage the pain, he'd take any luck tossed his way.

Several breaths later, he dropped the cloak. "I see you'll be the one we need."

Her hands dropped from the defensive stance and she cocked her head to one side. "I thought I *kneed* you?"

He ignored her smirk and restrained his comeback with an ability borne from long practice. "If you'd deign to follow me this time? People are waiting."

A heavy, dramatic sigh gusted from her. "I live to serve." The words had come with what appeared to be well-exercised sarcasm when dealing with superiors.

"I doubt that," he murmured. The words had no more than left his mouth than he wanted them back. Since he'd accepted the job three years ago, Talia hadn't been able to get a rise out of him, yet in minutes, this woman managed to shake him from his implacable demeanor.

The momentary surprise at his reply had been worth the slip —adorably pink lips poised for another snarky remark but nothing emerged. Without another word he stepped to T-intersection's blank wall, suppressing a wince at how his balls protested being jostled at all.

A panel dissolved and he stepped through, pausing for her, as he had earlier. When she hadn't shown, he'd stepped back out and waited. And waited a bit more. Then his little game had backfired. Why he thought he could or should play a game on her, wasting precious time, mystified him. He put that item in the 'To Consider After the Examination' list he'd mentally compiled.

She followed him this time, and with a rush of air, the panel reappeared behind them. She moved to pacing at his side. A soft whistle sounded from her. "Dang. Is this where my Clan money goes?"

As opposed to the sterility of the lobby area, the corridors were carpeted, the walls made of stainless steel and glass panels inset with glass doors.

He didn't miss a step as he automatically shifted to his administrative role. "We use little actual Clan funds. We take the money from the criminal element and when we aren't able to return it to the rightful owner, NACS is allowed to put the money for security purposes." He warmed to his topic, proud of the agency and the people he headed. "We are the smallest line item for NAC, but have one of the larger budgets of any of the Directories. In fact—"

"I'm not here for the quarter tour." She'd halted in her tracks and tossed her long, thick braid over her shoulder, forcing him to stop as well. "Look, I'm not a Council auditor. I'm here to do a job. The faster you tell me what it is, the faster I can get started, and the faster I can get to my vacation."

His teeth set on edge. He took a slow, calming breath and pushed his simmering irritation down. "You're the one holding us up. First you didn't follow me earlier. If we'd kept walking, we may have even completed your task by now." There. That logic should do it.

"If you hadn't played hide and seek—"

"That's enough." Only by the widening of her eyes and the heads popping out of the office doors like sideways gophers did he understand he'd roared the words. He composed himself, pulled the annoyance back and shut it in its box. Dammit. In less than ten minutes, she'd had him acting like his father.

"Is that supposed to scare me?" Her tone dripped with insolence and she widened her stance, preparing to strike if needed.

He cleared his throat. "My apologies. Won't happen again."

She jerked a nod and dropped her fighting position.

"If you'll follow me."

Without a word she turned with him and they continued marching down the hallway. Nathan Hebert could've at least revealed Chip's gender. Cal wouldn't have looked like such an idiot.

Why would it matter? He'd been wrong before and owned up to his mistakes. But this shifter female grabbed his attention the moment he entered the lobby. Her mahogany braid hanging to her waist, practically begging him to pull it apart. Her athletic build, light and trim, built for the run, built for the hunt. The steady pulse at her neck of thick, rich blood, and a curious perfume of flowers. Full, pink lips on that smart mouth. Pert nose to match.

Huge green-gold eyes that warned him to fuck right off.

He stifled a curse. The petite wolf shifter could only be trouble, in all capital letters. He shoved his thoughts back to where they should be—what rode on this investigation. If their intel got it right, a cabal was moving to take over the North American Council and reveal the existence of the entire paranormal world to humans, using the cover of the Pure Paranormal Movement.

This conspiracy needed to be nipped in the bud. Now.

After several turns and hallways, he came to his destination.

The Morgue.

Since she didn't want the 'quarter tour,' he let her figure out her location by the plate on the wall. He took a quick glance from the corner of his eye.

Her nose wrinkled, but the expression had been fleeting before the half-sneer returned. She didn't need the sign. The smell must've been enough.

He pushed one of the swinging doors open, gesturing for her to proceed him. After a slight hesitation, she complied.

The scent of antiseptic and magic overlaid the miasma of decay. He strode forward, past the row of chairs, then through the door from the waiting room into the administration area. He headed down the industrial white corridor with its over-bright lighting toward the examination rooms.

As they passed one of the offices, Monica Beauchamp, the Medical Examiner, glanced up from a microscope. "Hello Director." She waived a blue-nitrile-gloved hand in welcome.

A short indrawn breath next to him made him turn his head, but the Shifter's features had been schooled into a neutral expression. He returned his attention to Monica. "Good morning, Doc. How's Armand?"

"Still in Paris, visiting the grandmages." Her eyes grew wistful.

"You could've taken time to go with him." But he was relieved she hadn't. He needed her here to help with this case. An urgency had gripped him, pushing him to solve this quickly, as if the conspiracy began to come to a head. Though ruled by logic, he'd long-ago learned not to ignore his gut feeling.

"I'd rather not take time off now. Not with what we have on the table in there." She clucked her tongue. Then her eyes shifted to Cal's right and narrowed. "Is this the next of kin? Did someone identify the body and didn't tell me?"

"You run this place. Do you think I'm going to keep news like that from you?" He didn't wait for an answer, because he would absolutely keep information from her if he had to, and she knew it. "This is Chip Foster, the tracker from Hebert Security. Maybe we can learn more about the body."

Doc's dark eyebrows crept up her forehead. He could see the wheels turning in her mind, but she was far too polite to blurt out her surprise about the tracker's gender. She rose from her stool, came to the door, and presented her right hand. "I'm Monica Beauchamp, I run the Medical Examiner's office. Welcome to the Morgue. I've heard remarkable things about your scenting prowess. And any friend of Nathan's is a friend of mine. You're welcome anytime."

Chip's gaze flicked to him, with an expression he couldn't quite read. "Nice to meet you. You'll forgive me if I tell you I'd rather not come by if I can avoid it?"

This could be as close as an admission of weakness he'd see, that her sensitive nose took umbrage to the smells of death and decomposition, fear and sorrow. His heightened senses reacted enough to the odor. He could only imagine Chip's experience. *Surely that isn't her real name? Note—look up her real name.* He moved this to the top of his priority list. Well, to second, but more easily crossed off than figuring out the conspiracy. Plus, it would nag him until he knew.

Monica nodded as if expecting Chip's answer. "That's why we don't have any shifters in the office. Mostly Clan Magic and HP.

Should we get this over with?" She grabbed a file from the lab table where she'd been working and exited the room.

He allowed Chip to precede him. The denim followed her hips in a way his palms craved to shape. What *was* her name? He removed the mobile phone from the thigh pocket of his tactical pants, tapped on the screen, then typed a quick message. 'Prepare contract paperwork for Chip Foster. Advise when done.' He hit send. A thumbs up sign returned in a matter of seconds. Even if this turned out to be a bust and NACS didn't need her services, he'd have the information.

Good. He could put the stupid question to bed shortly. He should've done his homework—*had* someone do his homework—and he would've been prepared for all angles, including something as simple as her gender and her real name.

Doc pushed her way through the swinging door. The scent of antiseptic and death multiplied. "We do try to keep the smell at bay, but there's only so much magic can do," Doc said by way of apology to Chip. "I'd offer to blunt your nose completely, but you need it, unfortunately."

"I have ways of dealing." Her pinched face suggested maybe those ways weren't working too well.

Doc turned and pushed into another room, one with a single table. A sheet covered what lay there.

Magic washed over him as he entered, a waterfall of shivers pricked his skin. He had never gotten used to this, to the enchantments needed here. They kept all of their bodies separately. Years ago, magics timed to detonate hours after the body arrived at Enchanted Rock had killed one examiner and almost destroyed the morgue. They couldn't afford something like that to happen again. The smells were bad enough. From experience, he breathed through his mouth, taste buds would pick up some of the scent, but much less than his nose.

Doc stopped at the exam table, hands in her white lab coat's pockets, determination in her features.

"You okay, Doc?" Foster pulled up to the table across from the ME. She didn't look at the sheet, but stared intently at the woman across from her.

Doc turned with a wry smile at the ready. "Sure. It's just a shame what they did to this...person." She turned her gaze back to the sheet, the fabric glowing bright in the room's harsh light.

"So it's a person? HP or non-paranormal?" Had that been a tremor echoing in Foster's voice? Excitement? Or dread?

He crossed his arms and leaned a shoulder against the wall. The Medical Examiner could handle it from here. He'd already experienced the brutal glory once.

"I've said too much. I'd prefer you tell me what you find without any bias." Doc's hand moved to the top of the bulky form, grasped its cover, and dragged it down the body.

More precisely, what remained of it.

CHAPTER 3

Chip stifled a gasp.

Black and yellow and green oozed from countless places across what had once been a living being. What being, she couldn't be sure.

Yet. Doc had said HP. *Your nose knows.*

And the smell. She slammed the lid on her sense as much as she could, not that it helped much. The shroud must've been spelled, because the reek increased by several orders of magnitude once lifted. For a moment the wave crested, then fell back. She took a careful breath, drawing it through her mouth to avoid her nose as much as possible until she had to abuse the poor organ for purposes of the job.

She examined the body again. No skin remained. None. If left in the open, animals would've taken chunks, if not whole legs and arms. If in a closed environment, the skin would've been largely intact. But decomp was decomp. It followed mostly the same patterns. "I think this is only a couple days old. Maybe four or five."

"Your boss found him four days ago." Stavros said, a distinct note of irritation in his words.

So this was the body Nathan had found in the mechanic's garage. The one meant to terrify Nathan's girlfriend by making it appear as if Garrett Frazier returned. Clan Shifter had hoped to capture Frazier—or who they believed to be Frazier—before the leader of the murderous Pure Paranormal faction had an opportunity to announce his triumphant return. By Clan Shifter not notifying NACS about the possibility of Frazier's rising from the extremely dead, her boss had ruffled more than a few feathers.

At least she hadn't done the ruffling this time, even if it was her clan.

They should've known it couldn't have really been Frazier. Who can come back from a beheading by the Fae's Sword of Fallen Souls? She huffed a light laugh and immediately regretted it, as the hideous, slimy mess of scents entered her nasal passages, assaulting her brain in a jarring cacophony of reeks.

One struck a chord, but she held on to that for later.

If she had known what she'd be asked to do, she might've said no. She swallowed hard. No, she wouldn't have. Anyone who called for exterminating Human Paranormals—the so called 'leftovers'— so the four remaining Clans could be 'pure,' was someone who needed to be weeded out and banished. Anyone who killed HPs for the Pure Paranormal Movement needed to be exterminated themselves. If this body held a clue, she'd do this for days. Even if she had to show her weakness to the smug demon lounging in the corner.

"I'm going to need a bucket." Damn embarrassing for the best nose in the business to have a weak stomach, especially in front of the NACS Director. *You're such a dumbass.* How could she not have known his position? She didn't dare see if a smirk crossed Stavros's face. All of her concentration and willpower were required right now. Hopefully she wouldn't need it. *Yeah, right. This dude is juicy.*

Doc lifted a brow at her request, but crossed to a cabinet in the corner and removed a industrial gray bucket.

Chip took it from the other woman. She centered herself, then went to her mental box and took the lid off. Even without taking a new breath, the molecules remaining from the last inhale made her gorge rise.

Great. She forced the eggs and grits she'd had for breakfast back to her stomach. *Hold it together Foster. Not in front of the demon.*

She took a careful breath through her mouth. Taste buds and smell were linked, but it might—*Oh shit.* Breakfast rose again, and only by sheer will did she make it recede.

"Are you getting anything?" Doc asked, a furrow between her dark brows.

"Oh yeah, I'm getting—"She jerked the bucket to her face and heaved her stomach's contents into its depths. After the second wave of partially-digested eggs and grits, she snuck a peek to the Director. He better not be laughing at her.

His eyes had narrowed on her, no more. Good.

Another round came, then nothing remained. If she could've done this in private, it would've been better, but she knew not to ask to be alone with the body. Not only was the area probably subject to a camera system, so she'd be found out anyway, they would want witnesses to any non-NACS personnel working on the victim.

Doc handed her a couple of paper towels, probably taken from the dispenser on the wall, but Chip had been too busy blowing her guts into the bucket to notice. Next came a white cone containing water.

Chip wiped her mouth then rinsed, spit, and repeated. She didn't need her own body's reaction to interfere with her job.

Let's do this. She started at the head, gliding her nose over the crown of the skull, bone bright in the exam room's light between black bits of rotting meat. Nothing out of the ordinary here. A thin line ran across the forehead, around either side, to disappear around the back. "Would you remove the top of the cranium, please?"

The ME pulled the top of the victim's skull away, revealing the remnants of decomposing not-gray-anymore matter. They'd already extracted the bulk of the organ.

The tiniest bit of breakfast rebelled, but she kept the acid down. Nothing in the brain either. She shoved that one persistent scent back. She had yet to reach its source somewhere else on the body, somewhere she'd get to soon enough.

She nodded to Doc who replaced the cap. No ears remained. Chip skimmed along the temples, taking delicate sniffs, brain analyzing and categorizing the scents automatically.

Overwhelmingly, putrefaction in all its permutations dominated the odors. She began to isolate the sweet-foul organic molecules, push them into a mental corner, out of the way from the scents she'd need to examine further. Nothing along the eyes, either side of the head, where the nose used to be.

Then she reached the mouth. One of the scents she'd pushed back until she found its source hit her in the face. "Can you open the jaw, please?" She pushed her nose further in. Fillings. *In the teeth, eh?* If they were still in the vic's mouth, she'd stake her meagre savings the Medical Examiner hadn't found it. A little glow of triumph grew in her heart. At least all her puking hadn't been for nothing.

She continued down the right side of the body, working her way through the chest cavity and what remained. Then down to the feet, to reverse course back up the other side. "Would you hold open the incision?" She paused at what remained of the victim's intestines.

Weird.

Blood.

She moved on, continuing to the head. "Can you turn him over?" Whoever had skinned the body had left the sex organs to make the victim easily identifiable as a male. Why take the ears but not the dick?

Stavros, the NACS Director, grabbed a set of nitrile gloves from a box on the wall. Wow. Instead of calling an orderly, he helped Doc turn the victim over in a series of smacking and slurping sounds that did nothing for her stomach's desire to hold food ever again. Even her wolf whimpered a little inside.

Settle. She worked her course around the back side of the body. Once again at the head she straightened, an index finger tapping against her mouth. She slammed the lid on her senses, then re-examined the odors she'd discovered, turning them over and around and upside-down. Nope, she'd been right. Nothing remained to be discovered. At least for her nose.

"What can you tell me?" The slightest bit of impatience tinged Stavros's deep voice.

"Can we do this elsewhere?" She exited the room through the swinging door without waiting for an answer, headed to the Medical Examiner's office. Along the way her sharpened hearing picked up the slurps and slops of them turning the body over again. She shuddered, happy there was little left in her stomach to heave up.

Doc Beauchamp and Stavros met her less than a minute later, where she'd propped her shoulder against the doorframe.

The demon appeared deceptively calm, despite the frustration pheromones escaping his carefully-crafted shroud. Not many shifters would've been able to pick up on them. He must pay someone handsomely for *that* spell. "Do we need to go further out?"

She stared at him for a moment, stunned he had the courtesy to recognize the odors could overwhelm her, even from this distance. And that he hadn't made a wisecrack about her hurling up her breakfast made her re-examine him. Maybe he wasn't the asshole she'd thought. "Thanks, I'm good here. If I hadn't learned to put a lid on my smell-o-vision by now, I'd probably have gone feral and run into the wild, never to be seen again."

The slightest hint of a fraction of a smile came over his face. Or had she imagined the possibility of a sense of humor?

"Come on in and we can sit," Doc said. "Do you need anything? Water?"

Chip followed her to the small round conference table in the far corner and took a seat. "I'm good, thanks. I think the Director wants to get this over with."

Director. She wanted to melt into the cracks between the tile. How could she have thought him some admin person? The exam had taken her mind off her stupid assumption, but now it came back to smack her upside the head, like Aunt Hetty when Chip tried to steal a raisin-filled cookie from one of the cooling racks. They were always best stolen, and then eaten under the pier down the street from the house while staring at the sea. Her stomach perked up. Food later.

"Well?" He didn't bother to hide his impatience this time.

Crap. She shoved her reminiscing about her foster mother's cookies away and pulled the mantle of toughness back over her. She sat back and swiveled a bit in the padded rolling chair. "The vic was a male. At first, I thought Human Paranormal. I caught the whiff of magic specific to whatever being contributed to the HP's genetic background. At the time, I guessed demon. At least I thought he was HP."

Though she'd taken a casual lean in her seat, Doc straightened.

"Then when I got to the gut, I was confused about the decomposing blood in the intestines. I realized this wasn't an HP, but the scent of the original being—a demon—had been erased and replaced with the HP scent."

"Blood in the intestines?" Doc scribbled on a notepad.

"It was there. You would've assumed it was the victim's food, or maybe his own blood. But decomposing digested blood smells different than regular decomposing blood and different than decomposing flesh. By the amount in his system, and the lack of decomposing meat or vegetation, it figures he consumed only blood. That's the best I can tell you." Only Clan Sanguis, the demons and their made vampires, drank blood as sustenance. She snuck a glance at Stavros while Doc's pen scratched the paper. He watched her with narrowed, glittering eyes. Embarrassed to be found peeping, instead of moving her stare away, she turned her head to him, giving him the benefit of her next discovery with full eye contact. She couldn't afford to show any more of her soft underbelly. The vomiting had been enough.

His eyes widened a bit, then the corners of his lips lifted a fraction, an acknowledgement of her directness. But he remained silent.

Good. This next tidbit should be fun. "The second thing I found was fae gold."

Now he tensed. "Fae gold? Where?"

"In his mouth. Those fillings were probably part of why he was categorized as a human. None of the other clans would've needed them. He didn't either. But that's fae gold if I've ever smelled it."

Director Stavros muttered a curse and shoved one of his hands through his hair.

Huh. Such an emotional response from the stoic demon.

"I noticed he had a lot of fillings, and thought to have twenty-four filled with gold was a bit unusual," Doc said. "But sometimes humans just have bad teeth." She threw her pen on the tablet. "*Mierde*. I should've recognized this meant something and dug deeper. My apologies, Calum."

"None needed. I read your comments in your report, but the impact didn't register with me either." A muscle worked at his jaw, the only visible sign of his fury, probably directed at himself. Well, that and the sneaky pheromones he probably didn't know were escaping his shroud. Why did he stay so outwardly calm?

She could certainly understand the importance of the find. To have fae gold while not being of that clan meant the demon had done something monumental to obtain the precious metal. Maybe it had been stolen or had been given to the demon for a very important reason, because the fae wouldn't have parted with their most precious commodity otherwise. They'd have paid their debt in regular gold and not allowed the holder potential access to their realm. The fae preferred to stay stuck up in their own little world, eating sunshine and shitting rainbows, looking down their noses at the rest of the paranormal beings. Bringing in a non-clan member? A big deal. But how did this fit into the conspiracy?

What if those snotty fae didn't want to stay in their perfect little realm anymore?

"What did you say?" Stavros leaned forward, eyes narrowed like gray lasers on her.

Holy crap, she'd said that aloud.

He didn't give her an option to reply. He turned his attention to Doc. "Follow up on this and report anything. I don't care how small the detail." He didn't wait for Doc's reply either, swiveling his intensity back to Chip. "You. Come with me."

He pushed up from his chair and strode halfway from the room before Chip had gained her feet. She jumped up then hurried after him, despite her annoyance at being ordered around like a private.

What in the name of her wolf ancestors had she said to get that reaction?

CHAPTER 4

Cal slowed after the third corner to allow her to catch up. Foster shouldn't have to bear his poor humor. He swore to himself. Clan Sanguis. He had few operatives from the clan he trusted to take this information and make discrete inquiries in the demon ranks. All were out on assignment. Which left him.

He nodded to his assistant as he passed.

"The document is on your desk, as requested," Abraham said in his usual clipped, competent manner. He'd already gone back to his computer screen, no acknowledgement of his efficiency needed.

Cal continued into his office without breaking stride and continued to the opposite side of his desk. "Close the door then have a seat." He gestured to the leather chairs across the dark cherrywood slab from him.

The shifter complied, with the door, at least. From there, she moved to the tufted sofa against the wall to his right, sinking into the feather-filled cushions.

"Nice." She ran a hand over the soft leather that had cost him a pretty penny of his own funds. The way her nimble fingers stroked with appreciation made the blood rush to his dick. Dammit. He sat. How had this female worked her way past his defenses this fast? He cleared his throat and ripped his gaze from her hands to stare at the top of his desk.

No fucking at work. Scratch that. No thinking about fucking. At all.

Several moments later, the document his assistant prepared came into focus. The contract for Foster. He needed her for this investigation. The idea the fae may not be happy to stay safe in their realm any longer was the manner of thought he needed.

Clan Fae's NAC representative made Cal's security senses take notice. Zack's arrogance far surpassed the most arrogant fae and even that of a demon. And Cal's intel said something was going on in the Fae Realm. Once Simon de Vrys got back, he'd have to question him. Damn phones wouldn't work in the realm or he'd text his deputy. Cal categorized his idea of the fae representative as a possible suspect, one of many. But for now, he needed Chip for this part of the investigation.

He shoved aside the suggestive voice saying needed a whole lot more from her. No. This investigation only. If she worked out, maybe he could steal her from her private job at Hebert Security. Nathan would be pissed. Too bad.

He started at the top of the document and scanned through it. His eyes screeched to a stop on the first line. 'Moonlight Lily'? The beautiful, feminine name appeared out of character. He snuck a glance at the tracker, who'd reached for a bottle of water from the tray on the side table, but quickly pulled back when she realized he stared at her.

"What?"

"The water is there for the taking. Help yourself."

She pursed her lips, but took him at his word, snagging one, uncapping it, and taking a sip.

"Moonlight Lily, eh?" He cocked his head.

With green lasers firing from her eyes, she swallowed her mouthful of water, then placed the bottle on the coffee table.

Except it tipped over. Frozen for a fraction of a second with horror registering on her face, her features quickly morphed back to her sneer. "No one calls me that who doesn't live to regret it." She enunciated each word with as much contempt as could be jammed into it, rose, and opened the door at the far end of the sofa. She returned from his executive bathroom with a wad of paper towels several seconds later.

How would she know what lay behind the door? Ah, the nose.

She bent to mop up the water. Except the liquid had evaporated. She stopped mid-swipe.

"Cleaning spell. It's easier than allowing non-NACS personnel to have access." He shot a her a glance ripe with sarcastic humor. "It's a remarkably feminine name." And strangely suited to her and her remarkable scent. Wisely he kept that thought to himself. Her hard exterior compensated for the delicate beauty of the tiny shifter. He had no doubt she'd wipe the floor with someone who called her by her real name as she'd promised, let alone someone who called her 'tiny' or 'delicate'.

She crossed her arms, the leather of her motorcycle jacket creaking a bit. "Yeah, I don't care what my name sounds like. It's 'Chip' or 'Foster' to you and anyone else here. Are you going to cut me a check and I can be on my way, or what?"

Wolf packs generally went by alpha male rule, though a couple of packs did have female alphas. With her petite size, unusual for a wolf shifter female, he could only imagine how hard it would've been for Chip as a cub, then later as an adult. Because she was as alpha as any he'd seen. "No. No check. At least not yet. I think—"

"What the hell?" she exploded, her arms flying from each other, fists landing on her hips. "Nathan said this was a quick in and out. I'd be paid and on my way. I should've known better."

Mercenary. Disappointment trickled through him. A shame. But some of the best weren't interested in the cause of justice, just the money. "I can transfer funds today, if you like, and you can be gone." He kept going when she would've interrupted. "Or, I can double the generous rate we're paying you now to stay through the end of this investigation."

Her eyes had widened a fraction when he mentioned compensation, and she dropped one of the fists she'd planted on her hips. "Keep talking."

"I need someone with your skills, as this morning has shown. Nothing in this case is what it seems. Garrett Frazier is not Garrett Frazier. The HP in the morgue isn't an HP at all, but from Clan Sanguis." Wait a minute. "You don't vomit every time you track or use your smell senses, do you?"

She muttered something in a snarl he couldn't quite catch, despite his demon-enhanced hearing. "Could you repeat that?"

"I said, no, I don't puke my fucking guts out every time I start tracking." Her eyes flashed pure gold, predatory. The wolf in her must be close to the surface. "That was something few trackers could've done, let alone done without losing their lunch."

"Good. I didn't know if I'd need to be carrying a bucket around with me on the regular." As soon as the words were out, he cursed himself. Why did he feel the need to rile the shifter up? *Because you want a reaction.*

She glared at him. "Do I need to carry a stick around? You know, in case you forget the one shoved up your ass?" The quiet words said more than shouting.

Message received. He needed to give up the grade-school teasing. He gave himself a mental shake. Yes and no. He needed to act like the damn North American Council Security Director and leave a potential employee alone.

He schooled his features into their usual stony mask, picked up a pen and wrote in a figure on the contract. "Back to the original discussion. We will guarantee a week's compensation at double the rate. You may terminate the contract at any time. You have to sign it anyway to receive compensation for today. Initial next to the corrected rate, please." He spun the papers around and slid them across his desk. His gut told him he'd need her before the end of this investigation. While he believed in analytical examination, his gut was right more often than not. Therefore, he included it in his planning.

Rather than coming forward to sign the contract, she started pacing back and forth between the couch and the coffee table, muttering.

The urge to try to read her thoughts tugged at him. No. Many could tell when someone tiptoed through their brain. He didn't violate the trust of his employees that way and wouldn't do it to Foster. Even if she muttered to herself like she carried on a several-sided conversation.

Just when he began to question her sanity, she stopped. She lifted her gaze, even, unwavering. "I accept your offer."

The money won. Should he be relieved or disappointed? "Do you need to check with Hebert?"

She picked up a pen from the holder on his desk and paused her hand, the nib on the line. "No. I'm on liberty for the next two weeks. You can have me for that long."

His gaze had locked on her lips and mind leapt immediately to the gutter. *Damn, this female has wormed her way deep into you.* He shoved away the idea of exactly how he could have her. Strictly professional and by the book. And the book meant no sex with employees. If he repeated that to himself enough, the rule might stick. "Good. After you sign, please place a drop of blood in the square next to your signature."

Huge green-gold eyes lifted to his gaze. "Blood?"

"It's part of the standard contract. Nothing may be spoken about any part of this investigation to anyone outside NACS. The blood guarantees this."

Her lids narrowed. "What happens if I tell someone?"

"Pain. A sorcerer uses your blood to bind you to the agreement.

If you violate it, not only will we know, but we will find you while you're writhing on the ground in agony. I've seen a couple who violated the contract. The spell works."

She put her finger behind her. "That's bullshit. Why would you do something like that?"

"We have to work as a unit here with personnel from five clans, not all of which get along well at all times. If they went back to their clans and informed on everything going on, it would be... counterproductive to the administration of justice. Call your boss, if you need to. Hebert will tell you he made the same blood compact for his years of service."

She bit her lip, but kept her deliberations internal this time. Finally, her expression cleared and she nipped at her thumb with a bright, sharp incisor. A crimson drop welled instantly and she pressed it to the paper.

The aroma of her life's essence wafted to him and his head spun. Fuck. Nothing could've prepared him for her scent, let alone combined with her blood. Sweet and floral. Fire and passion. Unlike anything else he'd ever encountered, let alone anything he'd tasted. His fangs ached, begging him to feast. He turned to the window behind him, the large pane that looked out upon the central hall of Enchanted Rock, and tried to regain control of the unwelcome reaction. Shifter blood did nothing for demons or vampires. No sustenance. Why would her essence make him want to bite her neck and draw in the sweet...

He sucked back his fangs and fought to keep his breathing even. Desire for her blood, her body, rampaged through him. *No.* He would not give into the demon.

Finally, the multitudes—Sanguis, Shifter, HP, Magic and Fae—several floors down came into view. He concentrated on them going about their business at the North American Council or visiting or why ever else they were here. Anything to take his mind off the erection pulsing under his tactical pants' fly. After several more seconds, he grabbed the horns of the feral animal inside him and subdued it. He forced his face into a careful mask of calm, then turned.

Her head had cocked to one side, curiosity filled her eyes. "That's a really good cloaking spell you have there, demon. Do you mind giving a reference for the mage who created the spell? Hebert may find it handy at some time."

His heart stopped. *Demon.* He swallowed the ball stuck in his throat. "Why do you think I'm a demon? I could have bought a charm to make myself invisible. Any good practitioner in Clan Magic should be able to help you."

She crossed her arms, her jaw setting. "I wasn't talking about your ability to become invisible, but it was a clue. I was talking about the cloak you've put around your true essence. When you walked in to the waiting room, I thought you were HP. Hell, you even have the Clan's fae-silver medallion under your polo. I can smell it from here. But..." Her eyes widened and lips formed an 'o'. "You don't want to be known as a demon."

His thoughts whirled in his head, banging into each other in their panic. All the years his mother hid as an HP wasted. Every bit of gold paid to Clan Magic to hide him, wasted. No one had ever figured his secret. No one. The only one still alive who knew for sure was his father and possibly his personal secretary. And pops wouldn't risk the wrath of his brother-in-law, the King, by revealing a bastard demon son.

She put her hands up between them. "Look, it's none of my business what you want to do or what Clan you want to claim. How did you get into the HPs anyway?" She waved a hand in dismissal. "No, don't tell me. I'm here to do a job, I don't need to know anything personal about you."

He had a moment where he wanted to apologize when she appeared to be questioning herself. She didn't deserve it, but he couldn't afford his secret to be out. It was bad enough the body in the morgue may have been under the same spell, the spell no one thought possible. How many had access to it? Cal could be found out.

Get your shit together, Stavros.

He crossed his arms and pasted on his best glower, praying it would intimidate the shifter into silence. "You have no idea what you're talking about. I wish I had known this before you performed the exam and signed the contract. I would've asked for a different tracker. Someone who knows the difference between HP and demon." If only she'd been a regular human, he could take control of her mind and wipe the thought away. But none of the paranormal clans would fall for the demon glamour. He'd have to use what he'd been given by his mother, and the nuclear tactic would only draw this Shifter's anger.

She shook her head and jabbed her index finger at him, nearly touching his nose across the desk. "I don't run at the mouth. You need me to keep it on the Q-T, you got it. But don't pull this intimidation crap on me." Her irises had flashed gold again, and she panted in her anger.

As did he. His focused on the little breaths gusting from between her lush lips. His anger receded and he realized he was leaning over his desk, almost halfway, as was she.

Close enough to kiss.

CHAPTER 5

Chip jerked and took several steps back. She'd been in his face. His handsome, chiseled face, within reach of those gorgeous lips.

Not close enough, her traitorous wolf said. The canine prowled, wanting to get close enough to brush against the man's flanks.

Geezus. Who even used 'flanks' anymore?

Me. Want him. Her wolf rumbled her frustration deep in her throat.

No complications. Not now. Chip shoved her wolf into the back of her mental storeroom. Way in the back, where she should stay, then slammed the door.

She chanced a peep from between her lashes and found the flames in Stavros's pupils had faded away. That, with his cloaking ability and his wood-smoke scent. Oh yeah. Clan Sanguis for sure.

So he didn't want to be known as a demon. Not like she didn't have her own secrets. Let him have his bit of mystery.

She could play nice when she wanted to.

Or, pursuant to the contract she'd signed minutes ago, she could walk away now with guaranteed NACS funds and find a beach somewhere with a lot of fruity drinks topped by colorful little umbrellas. Maybe a boy toy to scratch the itch this male demon caused. After all, it'd been a couple years.

Yet, she would see this investigation through. Not like she didn't have reason to want to make sure any remaining Pure Paranormal assholes got what they deserved. Hetty deserved every effort Chip could put toward ending that nightmare.

"Look, I may have been wrong," she said through clenched teeth. "Even if I wasn't, it's none of my business. Whatever I've said in this room, will stay in this room. I give you my word." At least her word counted for something.

Beyond her nose, her reputation was all she had left. No pack to vouch for her. At least none she'd claim.

He crossed his arms, his black eyes examining her thoroughly, as if seeking out a trace of deception anywhere in her being. Skepticism morphed to decisive. "Very well. I will forward the contract to Personnel. Do you have a place to stay at the Rock? We have visitors' quarters in NACS, if you need them."

She hadn't thought the job would last more than a day, especially since she tended to piss people off with her attitude and inappropriate humor, so she hadn't arranged for a room in the Shifter section. She lifted her chin. "I'll take the quarters here, thank you." *Lookit you. All nice and such.* Aunt Hetty would be proud.

"Good. I have a feeling we will need your services soon and I'd rather have you close by."

His words made her stomach clench with the possibility behind his words. Well, not her stomach exactly. *Dammit—get back in your closet.* Her traitorous wolf did as bid, but huffed with humor as it sauntered its way back.

"As for NACS, I expect everything to adhere to regulations." He opened a drawer, pulled out a book, and tossed it across the desk. It landed neatly in front of her. "I expect you to get through the NACS Manual as soon as possible."

Her eyes strayed to the tome as thick as her wrist. Aunt Hetty's laugh echoed in her mind. Chip never had been one for following rules. Besides, that book would take any normal being days to complete. "All of it?"

"All of it. Tonight."

She bit back a whine of annoyance. "Very well." *What he doesn't know won't kill him.*

"Good." He hit a button on the telephone sitting on the desk to his right. "Abraham?"

When no response came, he looked at his watch, then a calendar open on his desk. His lips flattened for the barest moment. "Since my assistant had to leave early today, I'll escort you down to Quartermaster for your uniform and housing." He picked up the contract, then rounded the desk and headed for the door. "Don't forget your manual."

She snatched the hefty book from his desk. *Uniform?* She'd have to wear the same boring black BDUs and black NACS logo polo shirt? She hadn't even brought an extra set of clothes. Would they have anything small enough for her? Most paranormal males were big and muscular. Most females too. Her gaze strayed to how the BDUs fabric fit Stavros's muscular ass to perfection. How the polo stretched across his broad shoulders and biceps. A delicious shiver thrilled through as her wolf chuckled suggestively.

Stop it. Or no running for a whole week.

Her wolf pouted a bit, but faded from her conscious.

Dang it. Not running for a whole week would kill her. But this demon had captured too much canine interest. Her gaze strayed back to Stavros's ass. Caught too much of her human side as well.

Outside the Director's office, the older gray-haired man who'd been sitting at the desk was gone, light over his credenza turned off. Stavros laid the contract in a wooden organization box that bore the tag 'Personnel'. As soon as the document settled against the wood, it disappeared. A magic link to the department. Clever and organized.

She slid a peek at Stavros. He couldn't be that much of a jerk if he gave his people time off, like he'd offered the Chief Medical Examiner. Chip picked up her pace as he traversed several corridors. She wouldn't need to exercise today if he kept this up.

A phone's *ding* chimed. Not hers. If it were a text, a wild metallic honking noise would've sounded. A claxon loud enough to signal a nuclear launch heralded incoming phone calls. His tones? By the book. And utterly boring.

He pulled the phone from his BDU's thigh pocket, stabbed a large, blunt finger at the screen, and continued to read while he walked. He stopped, brows crunched together, lips a hard, thin line. Really, this guy needed to lighten up.

Since she had no idea where they were headed, she halted as well. All these damn hallways looked alike, same carpet, same paneling. If she had to, she'd use her nose to navigate the maze, but couldn't they afford to put up some signs?

"Come on." He pivoted and started running back down the way they came. "Back to the Morgue," he said over his shoulder.

Her stomach clenched. It must be bad if he got this worked up. "What happened?" she asked as she sprinted next to him.

"The body disappeared."

"What?" She winced at the rise in her tone and picked up her pace.

"I thought shifters—especially wolf shifters—had really good hearing." He'd murmured barely loud enough for her to catch the words.

She might've laughed at the bit of snarky joshing, but the body disappearing?

Several more turns and long hallways brought them back to the Morgue. She started breathing through her mouth, and not merely because she'd been running full-tilt and was a bit winded.

She'd been to plenty of morgues, both human and paranormal in her forty-three years, but, by her faithless ancestors, this place had the most foul combination of chemicals, decay, and used magic Chip ever encountered.

They continued past Doc's office, empty, yet the lights were still on. She must be in the exam room. Chip gagged a little. Dammit. She'd gladly take the mage's offer to blunt her senses if offered this time. Bangs and thuds echoed from the exam room down the hallway.

Stavros shoved open the door and entered, Chip hot on his heels.

Despite being told earlier the body had disappeared, Chip gasped.

Doc, bits of her hair dragged from its bun, tended to a male, shorter than Stavros, but even more thick and solid. His lab coat sported smudges of black and his hair stood on end. Chip had seen the deep, raven-black before. Gargoyle. He wore nitrile gloves and held a wad of paper towels dotted with a deep blue substance —blood—from his forehead with one hand while Doc applied a bandage to his face. Something bad must've gone down to wound a Gargoyle. Their skin resisted all penetration, except for fae silver.

The sheet lay tangled against the wall to her right, also bearing dark smudges. The stainless walls and table didn't seem to have sustained any damage. Chip digested the scene in less than a fraction of a second.

From his position next to her, Stavros threw up a hand, barring her from continuing further into the room. "Hold up. Monica?"

Doc's gaze didn't stray from attending to the gargoyle. "It's safe. As far as I can tell," she said bitterly.

With those words, he dropped his arm, but didn't continue into the room, so Chip stayed put next to him as well. She laid the heavy manual on a counter next to her. Best to have her hands free. Things had gotten pretty freaky around here. Wait a minute. Could Stavros even fight? He could be a pure administrator, without training.

"Schofield, what happened?"

Monica waved a hand at her boss, concentration furrowing her brow. "He can answer in a minute. I'm trying to remove a bit of--"

The gargoyle called Schofield slapped her hand away and pushed her hard into one of the cabinets against the far wall. His skin turned green, and his fangs descended. He threw his head back and roared, the echo beating against Chip's eardrums.

Shit. Chip coiled to jump forward. If she could get between the two...

Before she could move, Stavros cleared the exam table in one leap. He tackled the raging gargoyle who'd charged Monica, granite fists raised toward the groggy mage trying to regain her feet.

Chip sprinted forward, grabbed Doc's arm, and shoved the recovering ME behind her while Stavros struggled with the enraged fae. Stay and guard Doc or help the Director? There wasn't much room.

"Stay with Monica," Stavros bellowed. He began to get the upper hand, so Chip remained in place, guarding the mage. After a minute that seemed to last years, the director had the fae pinned on the floor, snarling, drool dripping from his lethal fangs. Stavros snapped restraints around Schofield's wrists at the small of his back.

The ME came around Chip, hands glowing. Chip put a restraining hand on the woman's arm out of an abundance of caution. "Wait."

"No, this has to be done." Doc's jaw set and she crossed the short distance to crouch next to Schofield. Over the place she'd been doctoring before, she put her hands just above the skin.

Schofield screamed. Not fury, but in agony. Though Stavros

had his knees on the gargoyle's back, the male bucked like a prized rodeo bull.

"What do I do?" Chip had to shout over Schofield's bellows.

"Stay there," Stavros said. Personnel are on their way. You're backup, in case something else attacks."

The doors burst open behind her and she spun to confront the threat, ready to show she may be a runt, but she had many cans of whup-ass in her arsenal.

Two uniformed NACS officers rushed in, one a muscular demon, the other a tall, red-and-black-haired female from Clan Magic. They gave her little attention, continuing to the threat.

The female motioned with her fingers and a lasso sprung from her hands to wrap around the legs, then tied off to the table on one side. She attached the other end to a handle on the wall which appeared out of nowhere. The officer promptly sat on the gargoyle's legs as further restraint.

The demon grabbed the gargoyle's head with both massive hands.

"Keep that right cheek where I can get at it, Berith." Doc inched forward, hands pointed at the wound. "Steady."

For several moments, nothing happened as she chanted indecipherable words. Chip could barely hear her over the gargoyle's snarls and howls. Then Doc rose, backing up with hands cupped into a ball, moving as gingerly as someone walking with a hundred-year-old stick of dynamite. She glanced at Chip, then nodded at the cabinet in the corner. "Grab a crystal exam jar, please."

Chip ripped open the door and grabbed a clear, thick-walled glass jar with a screw-on lid of the same material. "This?"

"Yes. Open the top and hold it far away from you. I'm going to have to slam my hands down, so brace yourself and be ready to put the lid on immediately before it escapes."

What in the hell did she have in her hands? Nerves jittered around Chip's stomach as she readied herself.

Doc extended her palms over the container about a foot and took a deep breath. "I'm going to do it on the count of three. One. Two. Three." The edges of her glowing hands slammed down on the edge of the glass.

Something *tinked* and Chip covered the top with the reaction speed given to predators. More *tinks* sounded as the thing began beating against the glass, trying to get out. Pure reaction had her hold the jar at arms' length.

"Screw the top on, dear." The ME sagged against the metal table, hands propping her up, panting. Any effort to contain her hair had been destroyed. Silver and gunmetal strands hung in disarray, obscuring her face. "Is he okay yet?"

The sounds of struggles had diminished, but snarls and thumps continued. Stavros rose and said, "Not yet. Captain Berith, can you and Officer Sand take him down to the med ward? I'll grab a gurney. Here, take my place," he told the uniformed demon. In three long strides, Stavros exited the doors.

Chip tightened the exam jar's lid then held the clear container up to her eye. A jagged piece of metal zoomed around the small space like an infuriated hornet. She shivered. "Can it break the glass?"

"Not that one." Doc straightened and shoved her hair out of her face, looping it behind her ears. The strands began to work themselves back into the bun of their own accord. The ME offered a tired smile. "At least I hope not. It's pure crystal, with the best containment spells available."

"What is it?"

"If I had to guess, it's fae silver. It's the only thing I know which can penetrate a gargoyle's skin." Doc plucked the jar from Chip's fingers, straightened her glasses, and examined the tiny metal fragment, which seemed to only madden it more. The *tinks* increased until it sounded like sleigh bells. Doc's brows came together. "I've never seen a gargoyle go green like that. The silver's spelled for sure. I'm going to have to do some research."

She crossed to a small door on the wall labeled 'CONTAINMENT' and pulled on the steel handle, revealing a foot-square recess. Doc placed the glass container inside and shut the panel, her face a mask of pursed lips and faraway eyes.

Wow. All this on the job's first day? Maybe all of the personnel here weren't stuffed-shirt bureaucrats.

Stavros returned with the gurney. After they'd loaded Schofield, he turned to the ME.

"Doc, why don't we get you a cup of tea and a chair, then we'll discuss what in the hell just happened."

CHAPTER 6

"I've never seen anything like it." Monica lifted her eyes from the swirl of milk she added to her cup. "And after fifty years in this office, you know I've seen some things that would make dragons give up their stash of gold to wipe their memories clean."

True. Just when you think you've seen everything, a berserker bit of metal turns a gargoyle into the Hulk. Cal learned years ago if he thought he had it all figured out, he'd get blindsided by a freak something or other. Any good plan prepared for all eventualities, including the flexibility for those you hadn't considered.

"I asked Schofield in to remove the fae gold in the decedent's teeth. I thought maybe we could do something with it, test it, whatever. Everything was going well, until the last tooth on the upper right side. Then—bam!—the body started shifting appearance, then exploded. I stepped back, trying to shield us, but I didn't get to the spell in time. Schofield bore the brunt of it, including that piece of metal." She shook her head. "The gold must've cloaked the fragment from our spell protocols. I was trying to pull it out when you two came in. Whatever it is, it's malicious. To turn Schofield like that..." Her fingers clutched the mug as her eyes widened. "Ooh! The whole thing should be recorded on the surveillance system."

Doc shoved her chair back from the conference table and rose.

He ground his teeth, cursing silently. With all of their planning, their precautions, and superlative personnel, nothing should've gotten through. Could this be part of the plot to overthrow the council? He'd suspected something with the reappearance of Garrett Frazier. With all the spells and protections after NAC put the leader of the Pure Paranormal Movement to death, nothing should've been able to come back, not even death himself. It concerned him that whoever pulled the strings hadn't awakened the toxic movement within the overall paranormal community. When combined with the killings and terrorizations, like what had been done to Carrie Fletcher, it led Cal to believe another reason existed for the conspiracy. Alannah Johnson had been keeping the various clan leaders off his back, but they were chomping at the bit to excoriate him for not solving several murders of prominent clan members. They'd been keeping the murders quiet too, fearful of destabilization within their own clans. Who would benefit from such activity?

Moments later, Monica returned, laptop in hand, then took her seat, entering logins and passwords.

While she navigated the myriad of security features, he studied the wolf from the corner of his eye. A cool one. She'd protected Doc, then helped get whatever the hell the tiny thing was into a safety container, capping it so fast her movements blurred.

Her gaze lifted and tangled with his for a heartbeat.

The moment stretched. *Say something.* "Good work, Foster. Most people don't get that much action the first day on the job. Or handle it as well."

The faintest tinge of pink lit her cheeks. "Thank you. For the record, I wasn't sure the NAC Security Director would actually be able to defend himself. I thought Directorships went to pencil-necked paper-pushers, not someone who could subdue a bespelled gargoyle all by himself."

A compliment? Even wrapped in the backhand, the words surprised him.

"Here's where we were extracting the gold," Doc said, rotating the computer so both he and Foster could view the footage. Monica rolled her chair toward him, forcing him to slide close to Foster so all could see the screen.

He tore his eyes away from the shifter to the surveillance footage where Schofield used his gargoyle heritage to make the gold come to him, tooth by tooth. "Were you expecting something?" Cal asked. "Why didn't he pull it all at once?"

Doc paused the feed and shrugged. "I thought placement might mean something. Sometimes you don't know what you don't know."

"Ain't that the truth," Foster muttered.

The video continued for a couple of minutes, the other medical examiner calling the gold to him, Doc bagging and tagging the evidence per procedure. Until about five minutes in. The body began to shift to its true form. As she'd mentioned earlier, Doc took a quick step back, hands glowing, but too late, the camera feed went white for a moment. When the video came back, the body had disappeared and both Doc and Schofield were picking themselves up from the floor.

A part of his brain remained stuck on the face of the demon on the table for a fraction of a second prior to the feed going out. Cal's jaw clenched. It couldn't be. "Play that back slow. Stop when it shifts back to demon form."

Doc hit the reverse, then slow-mo'ed the action at the last tooth. The body flickered like one of the early silent movies. And then there he lay. Full skin. Hair. Ears. Nose. She paused the video.

Grigori.

His half-brother.

Fuck. He stared at the demon's face, took in the cruel surfer-boy features, blond hair, perfect nose, and a sneer, even in death. How had his brother gotten mixed up in this? Cal rubbed a hand over his face. Like Grigori wouldn't jump at the chance for more power? To abuse more people?

"Isn't that the Demon Lord Counselor Raum's son?" Doc murmured. "After his trial, I thought he'd been released into the Councilor's care and been forbidden to leave his compound."

"That's right." Cal's voice sounded rusty. How Grigori had gotten a light sentence after what he'd done mystified many. Ten years ago. The story of forty humans murdered, drained dry and left stacked like cordwood in a Malibu beach house had made the human national news and riled up support for those wanting to keep the laws intact—no interference in the human world. And to get that sentence? *When your uncle is Clan Sanguis' King and your father has enough gold to buy his way into the royal family... Double fuck.* What if his own father was caught up in this? He'd always been an asshole. Now, by Grigori's escape, his father could be implicated in this conspiracy as well.

Cal couldn't be more satisfied.

"So, this was a Trojan Horse? To get to NACS?" Foster sat well back in her chair, her lips set in a hard line as she stared at the screen.

Doc's phone rang. She looked at the device and said, "Sorry, I need to take this. Hi, *cherie*." She left her office, shutting the door behind her.

Good. The ME didn't need to hear his plan.

"Grigori would not have been a willing sacrifice," he said to Foster. "I see a couple of options. I know Grigori's character. He was a narcissist and cared only for himself. He enjoyed inflicting pain on others. And he didn't like consequences. I could see him getting involved with a group looking to take over the North

American Council and reveal paranormals to the rest of the world. He would find the concept thrilling, being able to openly subjugate regular humans." He paused for a minute as she digested the information. If she asked, he could cover his knowledge of Grigori's background with the fact he'd been an officer at NACS during the investigation which lead to his half-brother's banishment.

"I can also see him either pissing off those in charge or screwing up," Cal continued. "He liked killing and pain too much. Wouldn't surprise me if he had gone a bit too far and became an example for those around him. Besides, who would say he disappeared, my—Councilor Raum?" he corrected hastily. Dammit. He was Human Paranormal, not Clan Sanguis. No more slip ups. "*Raum* couldn't afford to announce he'd not fulfilled his promise to keep that monster in his villa."

Foster sat quiet for a moment before she tore her eyes from the screen. "You said there are a couple of options. What's the second option?"

He shouldn't have used the phrase. "It's an accusation I'm not ready to level yet."

"Why not?"

Why not? With a nascent plan coming together, one which involved her, she'd need to know all the details. "I'm taking your word you don't run your mouth. This is for your ears only."

Her lips twisted and she folded her arms. "Thanks, I think."

"It's possible Councilor Raum may be part of the conspiracy. Politically, NAC is fragile. With Chairperson Beneman's murder last year going unsolved to date, it's been tough, especially with the Pure Paranormal Movement lurking in the background. Alannah Johnston has worked wonders keeping the fractured Clan Council together. Toss in an allegation against the Clan Sanguis King's brother-in-law, and it may upend her negotiations. The pact between Sanguis and HP has lasted almost a thousand years, and demons rely on their HP brethren to keep the smaller

Sanguis clan safe. Privately, there are many who believe demons shouldn't have to live undercover. That all the clans, minus HPs, of course, should take their place as the top predators on Earth."

"That's bullshit." The words burst from her. "Humans would probably hunt us all down and make us their slaves. Nothing like a bunch of panicky people to make them want to exterminate the Other." She used air quotes around the last word. "And we're as Other as it gets. You *have* seen District Nine, right?"

He huffed a sardonic laugh. "Exactly." Smart lady. His plan started clicking, pieces dropping into place like a puzzle. With each piece his irritation grew, even with its logic.

"You look like you're about to rip someone's head off right about now. You realize I *will* fight you." Her eyebrow arched with the sarcastic comment.

He reined in his temper. It would have to be him. Who else of all the demons in the agency could get into Raum's compound and question him? His son, that's who.

"It comes down to this," he said. "We have to go to San Francisco to determine if Grigori acted without Raum's knowledge or if the Lord Counselor is neck deep in the plot." Cal hoped for the latter. Finally, his father would get what he deserved, or at least a bit of his own back. "I need someone not known to many people of the NAC community to go with me. You'd fit the bill."

Her eyes narrowed. "Why me?"

He stopped the admission tipping his tongue. Why would he tell this woman? Because he trusted her? Too soon for that, but as a contractor, she'd signed her oath. Plus, she'd indicated she didn't want to hang around afterward. And with the short bio he'd gotten from the phone conversation with her boss yesterday, Foster could work undercover.

Logical.

"Why do I need you? Cover. I'm going as a demon. And we may have interaction with the Court." For a moment, the words stuck in his throat before he forced them out. It was his only option, after all. "You were right. I am of Clan Sanguis. If I go without someone to feed from, they would assign me a slave for the duration."

Her face turned bright crimson, then she shot up, her finger pointing at him. "I am not going to be your damn blood slave. You are *not* drinking from me." Her chin jutted forward. Quick breaths made her chest rise and fall with her agitation.

"I never said I'd drink from you. You *do* remember demons don't get sustenance from anyone other than HPs or real humans, right?" She settled a bit, so he continued. "One, I use stored blood. Two, you're smart and can pick up on things I don't see. You have superior smell, slightly better hearing, and great eyesight. They will underestimate you because of your size and your status, especially when I introduce you as an HP. Hebert said you can take care of yourself in a fight." He cocked a wry brow. "I tend to believe him."

She'd relaxed a bit from her aggressive stance and sat, but skepticism still tilted her head and made her sight down her nose. At least she was listening. "No drinking."

"Got it. No. Drinking." When she still seemed dubious, he said, "I would like to stress the importance of this mission. It could mean the difference between our world as we know it and a world where paranormals have taken over, which we've already identified will have one of two bad ends. Either they'll subjugate the world's human population, probably leading to mass murder and enslavement, or, the paranormal world will be subjugated to the human. Possibly wiped out. I don't have anyone else I can trust to bring with me." *Please say yes.*

Her eyes narrowed. "You *trust* me?"

Maybe not enough not to kick me in the balls. Though he had kind of deserved that one. "I trust you'll live up to your contract. I trust you when you said you don't run your mouth. I trust your sniffer is the best in the business. I trust that you have no love for Pure Paranormals, so if there's reason to believe one of them has joined the conspiracy, you will want to ensure justice is served. Is that enough?"

For all the hastiness Nathan described in Chip Foster's personality, she took what appeared like hours to make her decision. "Fine. But don't think I'm staying if I don't like it. It says in the contract I can leave at any time."

"That works for me." But really it wouldn't. He shoved aside the part of him who wanted to grab her, sprint into the night, and concentrate on how to make sure she stayed.

Doc entered her office, tucking her phone back into the pocket of her lab coat. "What'd I miss?"

"Not much," he said.

Only him admitting his deepest secret to someone he barely knew, someone he had an unexpected and inappropriate need to bury himself in, someone who could either make or break this investigation to the ruin of the North American Council.

No. Doc hadn't missed much at all.

CHAPTER 7

Chip threw the heavy manual across the room where it *thunked* against the wall. Who cared if a report had to be put into NACS JCS—their computer system—then cross referenced with clan security apparatuses for deconfliction? That the investigator had to knock on someone's door and announce they were there to arrest them before they could break it down?

Sure way to get your ass killed.

She shook her head and climbed from the double bed in the cramped room NACS offered. Lumpy mattress too. Some of that money that made the office space pretty could be used down here for bigger rooms, comfy-er beds, and a shower big enough to turn around in.

This was still a palace compared to where she grew up, sharing a three-bedroom house with at least ten paranormals from various clans. Only one bathroom serviced by a sporadically working water heater. Yet Hetty's bungalow beat what the street offered to clan runaways, danger and death if caught by paranormal smugglers. And the love. Hetty's heart had to be a hundred times the size of anyone else's. To be sucked dry by one of the very demons the generous woman helped, one who'd been mesmerized by the Pure Paranormal Movement... Fury began to rise. Enough.

Chip turned the hot water faucet to its maximum. The heavy spray emerged, steamy and scalding. She adjusted the temperature to her liking, a degree short of lobster-killing, and stepped in with a sigh of appreciation. As she shampooed and lathered, she fought against the visions of Hetty's sightless eyes and bloodless corpse.

The whole Rock should've run out of hot water by the time Chip stepped out. A thin, crappy towel did its best to remove the droplets from her pinkened skin. Once done, she wound the scrap around her. A quick wrap, and another tissue-thin towel bound her hair, soaking up the extra water.

As she hadn't shut the bathroom door, the steam made its way into the room, fogging up the low bureau's mirror. She reached into the closet for a hanger with a pair of dark skinny jeans, a purple silky blouse and her favorite black motorcycle jacket. She shrugged into the first two, both foreign garments purchased last night, then wiped a hand across the reflective glass.

Hmm. Not bad. But way too feminine. Give her a snarky graphic t-shirt, boot-cut jeans, and Doc Martins and she could kick the world's ass. She dropped to a deep knee bend. Meh. Enough stretch for her purposes, but the blouse? Nothing short of a miracle would get blood from it. From the corner of her eye she caught the digital clock.

Crap. Fifteen minutes.

Back to the bathroom and she finished her ablutions. What to do with her hair? Cool and trendy. She pictured the woman who'd sold her the blouse and jeans last night on the NACS credit card, then fashioned a bun low against her nape and to one side. On a whim, she teased a couple of strands to wisp around her face.

Quick makeup—blush, eyeshadow, mascara, also new. It's not

like she didn't know how. She chose not to. Men didn't take you as seriously if you wore the mask.

She stopped, caught by the reflection of the strange, sophisticated woman in the mirror. The urge to climb into her graphic tee and combat boots nearly overwhelmed her.

A knock sounded.

She ripped her eyes away from her gussied up image and dashed for the door. "Coming." She opened it, then turned around and dashed right back. Dammit. She still didn't have her shoes on. Her gaze caught on the bureau's top. Or the jewelry. Gah. It sucked being a girly-girl. Too much stuff.

She sat, zipped up one of her lavender suede ankle boots, stylish, but more sensible with a mid-wedge heel. "My apologies. I'm almost never late."

The Director didn't respond, so she looked over her shoulder. He stood just inside the door, an inscrutable expression on his face. He'd ditched the BDUs and agency-branded polo in favor of black chinos, black button-down, and a blazer. Dark demon chic. And damned hot against his golden skin.

"What?" she asked when he didn't respond. She shoved her foot in the other boot, zipped it up.

"Nothing. We have a timeline to meet, so we better not be late."

"Shit." She slid the jewelry into her palm. Oh yeah, her jacket. She grabbed it from the hanger and slid her arms in, happy it took her outfit from girly to edgy. She eyed what remained in the closet, a row of five NACS uniforms. At least she got to wear civvies on this operation.

"Nice to travel as rich people for once," she said.

"Hebert said you'd done undercover work before."

"Usually it isn't glamorous. More often than not, dive bars and seedy hotels." She tried to fasten the necklace, a 'statement piece' the saleswoman had called it, but her fingers kept fumbling.

"Here, let me." His fingers brushed hers and her breath hung in her throat. He worked the clasp, fingertips against her sensitive nape. His presence at her back and the heat radiating off him made her stomach flutter. Her body soaked in the warmth, urging her to lean into him. His hands stilled, then fanned across her shoulders, thumbs brushing light as a butterfly.

A tiny step back. All it would take, her wolf suggested.

To forget her promise to Hetty to get every Pure Paranormal bastard she could.

The flutterings in her stomach turned to lead. She stepped forward and snatched her purse from the bedside table, her travel bag with its new clothing from the metal luggage carrier. "Ready?" She schooled her face into its normal mask of insolence, then pivoted and started toward the exit with her packed rolling case.

He'd made his way to the door, hand on the knob. "I'm going to need a name to call you, other than Chip or Foster."

She stopped as she reached him. "Fine. What do you want to call me?"

"Lily."

Over her dead body. Hetty had been the last to call her by the name. "How about Tanya? I've used that before. "

"Why not Lily?"

Because that was my old life. And she still licked the old wounds. And the way he said it made her feel like a real female, not an androgynous security officer. "Because I prefer not to use the name. That's why."

"You're going to need something you answer to without me having to get your attention. I'm afraid I'm going to have to insist." The set of his mouth said he wouldn't budge.

Should she fight him on this? Not worth it. "Don't be surprised if I don't answer to that either. Lily or Tanya or whatever."

He stared at her for several seconds, as if trying to unravel a particularly complicated knot.

"I thought we're late?"

"Yes," he said simply, then hesitated. "Had trouble sleeping last night?"

She followed his line of sight to the floor where the NACS manual lay open and resting on pages, some bent. "It's a little dry."

The corner of his lips curled up. The smile transformed his stern visage, warming his eyes. As quickly as it came, the grin flew away and the autocrat returned. He led her to an elevator.

Of course she'd had a tough night. Her wolf kept bringing up the infuriating demon. She'd finally fallen asleep, only to have her first sex dream ever.

Featuring him.

All six foot plus of muscle, taut skin, and fiery need banked in his dark eyes. She'd woken on a strangled moan, so close to orgasm with what his hands and mouth had been doing, especially what his lips and tongue had done between her legs, she almost finished herself right there. But she'd stopped, despite the growl of frustration echoing in her head. Bad idea having fantasies about someone she couldn't and shouldn't have.

'Couldn't'? Because, while she respected his desire to reject any affiliation with Clan Sanguis, he was still a demon. One of the same clan who drained Hetty of her HP blood and discarded her. No demons for Lily. 'Shouldn't' because sleeping with someone she worked with screamed unprofessional. *Lookit you. Who's following rules now, Lily-girl?* echoed in her mind in Aunt Hetty's voice.

The elevator's doors opened and she stepped in.

He followed, leather duffle in hand, and jabbed a number on the panel.

Inside the metal box, his scent drifted to her. Rich. Smoky. Sexy. Her wolf leapt forward, inhaling the essence and wanting to rub herself in it, cover her fur with the smell.

No. Bad girl.

Her wolf whined.

If only she could distract herself somehow, like the way she'd cooled her overheated body by reading the NACS manual. She regretted not allowing herself the orgasm. The things he'd done in her dream, the things she'd done to him. Heat started up her neck. If she'd rubbed one out, maybe she would've been able to ditch the visions still dancing in her mind. Because following the rules never worked for her.

Her inner wolf yipped an agreement, turned twice and laid down, mahogany tail over her nose, gold eyes silently rebuking her.

The doors slid open and she exited the carriage behind Stavros. The giant black hole, easily three stories high, stared back at her. The shifting rainbow of color at its edges mocked her with the pretty hues.

The hair on her whole body raised in warning and she stumbled to a stop. "I should tell you I don't travel well by vortex. It doesn't like me." *It crumples me up, rolls me around and spits me out weak, panting, disoriented, and wanting to vomit.* She swallowed the acrid taste of bile.

"It doesn't like a lot of people."

"But—"

He laid a hand on her shoulder. "We're only going to San Francisco, so it should be a shorter ride."

"Okay." She swallowed, allowing him to lead the way. "It's you I'll be puking on anyway."

Officer Sand, the tall, red-and-black-haired member of Clan Magic from the previous day and the sole person in the transport area, stepped up. "I ensured no one else is in the bay, Director." She walked next to Stavros to a platform directly next to the vortex.

"Remember. If I'm not back tomorrow, give Council Chair Johnston the Priority One file."

"Yes, sir," Sand said with a crisp nod. She walked away and

entered the elevator. Chip followed the officer's progress. The doors slid shut in front of a troubled face.

His words echoed in Chip's mind, and a shiver slunk down her spine. Would anyone miss her if she didn't return from this mission? Would the Hebert Security team miss her? She'd been a pain in the ass to all of them.

"Lily?"

She turned. Stavros maneuvered her bag to the pad. And held a hand to her.

Wait. He'd called her Lily and she'd answered. His tone had been low and he slightly strung out her name as if savored. The word slid along her, like a caress against a silky coat. Her teeth ground. Fine. If he wanted to call her that, she'd take it for the time of the mission.

"Director." She accepted his hand, the feminine part of her she thought she'd erased delighting in the courtly gesture.

"It's Cal. Or Calum."

"You're going to use your real name?"

His mouth tightened. "The people we're going to talk to will know me and what position I hold. You're the undercover one."

With the slightest tug of his hand, he turned her toward the giant void. Fear flooded her heart. The last time she'd traveled by vortex, she'd been dizzy for a week. Granted, the trip had been a long distance, to the European Council in Poland. The overwhelming need to bolt nearly lifted her feet and sent her toward the elevator. She couldn't be that weak again. That vulnerable to anyone.

But Aunt Hetty whispered through her head. Only the vengeance in her heart kept her on the platform. She dove into the need for retribution, spread it across her body, until her fear had been washed away. "Okay. Let's do it."

"You sure? You're looking a little pale."

Fire lit her cheeks at his suggestion of weakness. "I can go home with a pocket full of NACS funds and finish my week sipping fruity drinks while y'all try to figure out what the hell's going on, *or*, we can get going."

A smile grew, revealing strong white teeth against his tanned skin. One that she felt all the way to her girly bits. "There's Lily. A fighter to the end."

His reaction confused her. "What—"

He grabbed her hand and sizzling electricity arced between their palms. He laced his fingers with hers. And pulled her toward the vortex, the portal that would carry them to San Francisco. "Don't let go."

"Wait. Don't—" She stumbled forward.

Too late. Her skin prickled.

A sucking sensation pulled at her head, wanting to leave her feet behind. Her wolf whined, then threw her head back and howled.

Surroundings faded to black.

CHAPTER 8

Lily gripped Cal's hand like a lifeline, when in reality she was his. He stepped into the portal, his surroundings twisted, swirled around him until they merged into black. The stream jerked him forward, tugging Lily with him.

If he was to tell the truth, Cal didn't like traveling by vortex either. The far ones, like Great Zimbabwe or Warwel Chakra, left him feeling stretched thin and with a need to feed. But the diversion to the closer North American ones like Tamalpais, north of the Golden Gate Bridge, were minutely better. Last night he'd hoped feeding double what he usually took would stave off the crash. Nope. His fangs itched to descend, to sample Lily's blood.

Or had the bagged blood left him more than enough sated and he wanted to sink his teeth into the feisty shifter while he sank his dick into her velvet warmth?

The few hours of sleep he'd gotten had been interrupted by the most erotic dream he'd ever experienced, far surpassing anything in real life. His hands had dominated her soft skin, mouth ruthlessly possessed the peaks of her beautiful breasts, masterfully tortured her pussy and clit until she writhed in the sheets, begging for him to enter her. In return, she'd conquered his lips, shattered him with her mouth on his dick, made him lose control. As he been about to sink his cock into her, he'd woken. Panting. Sweating. With a raging hard-on he'd had to relieve in the shower. At the time, he'd believed it had been enough to get her out of his system.

A massive miscalculation.

When she opened the door to her quarters, hair pulled up, loose and sexy, begging to be freed, with her curves outlined by her skin-tight jeans, he'd grown hard again. All the blood had obviously gone to his cock, or he wouldn't have stepped closer to fasten the necklace. At least she stepped away when she did.

He needed all of his attention on the mission. Not on a sexy wolf-shifter siren.

The vortex process began to reverse itself, mercifully pulling him from his thoughts, because his dick stirred yet again. Colors danced for several seconds until they pulled together into an understandable location, Mount Tamalpais Vortex, across the Golden Gate from San Francisco.

Lily still held his hand. Crushed it really, like if she let go she'd spin off into the universe, never to be seen again. A little green around the muzzle too. She held her fist to her mouth.

"You okay?" he said.

She swallowed hard and lifted stricken eyes to his. "I'm okay," she mumbled around her hand.

The small vortex held a NAC garrison. The security chief, a blond bear shifter the size of a small mountain, stepped forward and offered his hand. "Director Stavros. Good to see you, sir. I have a car waiting."

Cal took the shifter's hand with pleasure. Many people thought bears merely bulldozed their way through any situation, but this one knew how to use finesse when necessary, the bulldozer when all options failed.

"Aaron McClardy, Lily Foster. Aaron runs the Security Section for Mt. Tamalpais. Lily will be working with me on this assignment."

Aaron took Lily's hand, and uttered purely professional sentences of greeting, which she returned with a subdued courtesy Cal could hardly square with the Chip Foster he'd met yesterday. In character already or still dealing with the effects of vortex travel?

Aaron led them through the complex, much smaller than Enchanted Rock. Due to the time, three in the morning Pacific, and the back corridors Aaron used, no one would be any wiser of the Director's presence.

Cal and Aaron placed the bags in the rear of the waiting black SUV, while Lily climbed into the front passenger seat.

"You know where to find me if you need me." Aaron said, following him to the driver's door. "I'm fully staffed now. Thanks for fighting for me. We're finally starting to get a handle on the shifter trafficking problem."

"Good. You can only do less with less, right?"

A grin split Aaron's face between his golden moustache and beard. "You got that right, boss."

Cal slapped his palm on the shifter's shoulder as he shook the proffered hand, then slid across the leather driver's seat. He navigated out of the garage and began the ninety-minute drive to father's compound.

He ran the twisted mountain roads until he reached the Panoramic Highway, then he headed south toward a place he'd hoped never to visit again. Lily leaned her seat back a bit and appeared to doze. She'd been so subdued, more, he suspected, from the vortex trip than her acting. At least she'd lost the green tinge.

Which left Cal with his thoughts, none happy. More specifically, Lord Councilor Raum. He didn't relish the prospect of seeing his father after thirty years. The demon had tortured both him and Cal's mother, Nerissa. Initially, she'd mistaken Raum's attention for sincere love, and believed him when he said he'd petition King Krian for marriage, when all along, he'd been negotiating a marriage compact with the King's sister. When Nerissa found out about her lover's betrayal, she'd just learned of her pregnancy, a violation of clan regulations which said only the Demon ruler could approve procreation. She did the only thing she could've—fled the dangerous and violent Clan Sanguis where combat determined who was right and who was dead. The savagery burned in his gut.

Nerissa hid herself and her son, half of her fortune in gold spent on spells to hide their true nature. The other half went toward buying into the HP Clan through bribes to influential bureaucrats. Safety could only last for so long. Ten years later, Raum found them, and took them back to his lair. Cal's hands flexed around the steering wheel. Much tighter and he'd have snapped it.

Mom hid the violence from Cal. Raum raped her, took her blood by force, claimed her to be his mate though nothing could be farther from the truth. He used Cal's life as his bargaining chip to keep her compliant. Just as Cal hid the torture from his mother, and how Raum used her life to ensure Cal's submission. For years after Nerissa's death, Cal's existence in his father's home had been nothing but a cycle of abuse and misery until he'd attained adulthood and escaped.

And learned the truth. Raum had murdered his mother.

If Nerissa hadn't drummed a sense of lawfulness into Cal, he'd have killed the demon years ago, pursuant to clan law of trial by combat. But, 'Just because you can, doesn't mean you should' had been Nerissa's maxim.

He wouldn't sully her love and sacrifice, despite the revenge which still burned in his heart. His father hadn't shown up in any current NACS investigations—until now. Raum would finally be brought to justice. If not for Nerissa, for something.

Too soon, the hour and a half trip came to its conclusion. He parked in the driveway of a fifties ranch, a house he kept for emergencies. It sat on a large lot up in a canyon in the Pacifica hills. Game time.

Lily stirred when he cut the engine, smothering a yawn with the back of her hand. “We’re there? How long was I asleep?”

“About ninety minutes. We’re not there yet. This is a safe house I have in case of emergencies. It’s not far from Raum’s compound.” He opened an app on his phone and hailed a ride share. “We may need the car at some point, so we’re dropping it here.”

Lily met him at the tailgate and retrieved her bag. She’d grown even more quiet than usual, no smart quip at hand, perhaps sensitive to the tension bunching in his shoulders.

A few minutes later, the vehicle arrived, and minutes after that, rounded the hill to the next canyon, then up and up to the very top of the mountain. As the car made its way, dread wormed its way into his heart. He shoved aside the images crowding his memories and spied the tall metal gates regulating access. He punched the code on the security keypad, surprised it still worked. Most likely the combination alerted a guard of his arrival. It couldn’t be helped. Better to not be denied entry.

Cal’s stomach began to crawl as the three-story, stucco structure came into view. With its red tile roof, carved granite moldings, and grand, carved wood, double doors banded with wrought iron, it would fit perfectly into the Italian countryside as some centuries-old villa of the Borgia’s. The mansion even held its own set of dungeons, more cruel than any old Cesare could dream up.

Cal’s teeth clenched. He’d learned those cruelties all too well.

Once stopped at the doors, Cal removed the bags, then used the mental power assigned to all demons to control regular humans' minds. The driver would remember nothing of this trip or where he picked up his passengers.

"My Lord Calum?" A tall, thin vampire, his father's personal assistant for hundreds of years, strode toward them from the open door, a frown of dismay creasing his brow.

What he wouldn't give to separate the head from that bloodsucker's neck. "Good morning, Surgat."

The vampire halted several paces away and bowed deep at his waist. An exact count of three, then he rose. "Lord Counselor Raum is not in residence at this moment. Should he have been made aware of your arrival, I am certain he would have altered his plans."

Dammit. He'd hoped to surprise his father, but he didn't have the sources placed to make sure he'd be home. As one of King Krian's advisors, he traveled extensively and sometimes stayed with the court. Cal assumed the mantle necessary for the demon world, extreme arrogance. "I have need to speak with the Lord Counselor. When may I expect his return?"

Surgat's flicked to the travel cases next to Cal. "His schedule calls for him to return this evening. Would you care to wait?"

"If his household would be so hospitable." The formality at this level made his head ache.

"It would be the household's pleasure for you to stay. Please leave your bags here. I will have someone take them to..." His glance shifted to Lily, questioning her status.

"One room please. This is Mistress Lily, my pet. She will attend to any of my blood needs." He took her hand and glanced to her as if he felt affection for the woman he used not merely for sustenance, but who may be granted vampire status at some point.

At least her acting skills were up to par. No one would believe the adoring look she gave him wasn't real. Meanwhile, she crushed his hand to a pulp. He could only imagine the curse words she silently chanted at his use of the word 'pet'.

"Excellent, excellent," Surgat said, and led the way into the villa, Cal and Lily trailing.

At least his father's assistant had bought Lily as a human. No other paranormal, even Human Paranormals could be turned. Though HP blood brought a better meal, humans sill comprised the bulk of Clan Sanguis' blood needs.

As he ascended the wide stone staircase, several vampire servants whom he'd never seen before passed by. They bowed low, showing their respect for their demon lord's visitor.

If only they knew the truth. No mere visitor, but the bastard son. And not merely the bastard son, but now Lord Counselor's heir.

The irony. Cal been treated by his father as an afterthought, and been treated by his brother as an insect from which to pull wings. And now...

Even if his father could claim his bastard son his heir, Cal would never accept the role. His father's brutality in the way he and other lords maintained the stratified nature of the Demon Court made his skin itch. No one should have to live in fear of constant death for insulting someone or some arbitrary offense against the King. The clan's glamourous court hid a multitude of barbaric deeds.

He shook off the dark thoughts and focused on his surroundings. Nothing had changed in the grand entryway. Dark coffered ceilings above, while paintings of European masters littered the white plaster walls. Lily made a poor show of not gaping at the costly furnishings, art and tapestries. Or was her wonder part of her act?

Surgat continued into the courtyard contained by the four walls in the classic southern European tradition. The vampire wound through the enormous square villa's formal garden plantings, with its low hedges, sculpted trees, and central fountain, to the stairs leading to the second floor housing the family's quarters.

Though most wouldn't notice, the estate's level of care had diminished. Still pretty and ornate, the hedges weren't clipped as precisely, faded blooms littered the pathways.

Interesting. He made a mental note to request an analyst do a deep dive into his father's finances.

Cal scanned up to the open galleries used as hallways. No sign of hostiles. He settled a bit, but his alert status approached Def Con One.

Surgat led him and Lily up the wide stone staircase, then across the second-floor balcony. The assistant stopped at a magnificent set of double doors of carved wood. The guest quarters. Interesting. Probably not sure of Cal's status, so the sub-basement room he had occupied before could be seen as an insult. Best not to insult in the Sanguis world.

Cal should take to heart the example graven into the tall wooden panels—a passage familiar to many humans who believed in the Old Testament story of Adam and Eve with the Serpent coiled around the apple tree. Could there be any better warning about how he needed to watch his step in his father's household? Knowledge could lead to enlightenment...or treachery.

With exaggerated courtesy, Surgat threw the doors wide and with a sweep of his hand, ushered his charges through. "I trust this will be satisfactory, Lord Calum?"

Lily gasped, her eyes rounded with wonder.

Cal suppressed a chuckle, instead scanning the large, luxurious chamber as if he were truly assessing the appropriateness for one of his stature. The tester bed dominated the room, oversized and fit for a human king with its curtains at each corner hanging from the fifteen-foot, coffered ceiling. A jewel-toned rug almost the size of the room cushioned the stone floor. Enormous, hand-wrought tapestries spanned smooth plaster walls on either side of the bed. A seating area faced a corner fireplace, blaze alit.

Two oversized armchairs flanked a tufted leather settee. Grim satisfaction surged in him. Not a basement hovel.

"The rooms will suffice," he said, resuming the formality. It should. Lord Raum settled the visitors he wanted to impress in this chamber.

"My Lord Calum is most generous," Surgat said with a low bow, which reached the requisite level then rose right back. The acknowledgement bow.

Cal stifled impatience. The layers of etiquette in this place could drive anyone mad.

"Breakfast will be in one hour, if you would prefer the dining room. If you tell me her requirements, I can send your pet a tray for her nourishment." His gaze flicked to Lily, then back to Cal.

"I am perfectly fine with a cheeseburger and fries, thank you. I prefer my burger rare." Lily hadn't designed her sweet tone to cover the snarl.

Cal turned and took her hands, for all the world a demon inappropriately besotted with his pet, enough to not mind the strange breakfast request. Behind her eyes burned a fire no man could ever extinguish. "Surgat. I believe we will both be taking our nourishment in the dining room this morning. You may fix me whatever you serve my Lily."

Satisfaction glowed in her smile, which she promptly turned on the hapless assistant.

Surgat sputtered and squirmed. "But Lord Calum—"

"Oh, and I would love to see Lord Grigori." He'd turned to guage the vampire's reaction. "Will he be able to join us for the meal?"

The assistant's pale, thin face lost all color, as if he hadn't fed in months. "Uh, no. Lord Grigori is...under the weather right now and unavailable for visitors."

Right. Because he blew up in my morgue yesterday. Cal added every bit of hard patrician authority he'd learned from his father for his next words. "I will have to visit him in his room then. I take it he has the same suite?"

The vampire's eyes bulged from his head then darted in every direction as he tried to find a solution. He lifted his gaze again when he found it. "Lord Raum has directed he would have no visitors under any condition."

Cal stared at Surgat, using the same borrowed disdain, until the vampire began to fidget. Finally Cal said, "Very well. I will address the issue with Lord Raum. You are dismissed."

Surgat bowed, backing from the room, closing the doors behind him without a sound.

"Holy crap," Lily whispered. "What *is* this place? Feudal Russia? Is this Lord Raum like a tzar or something? Are we gonna get Cossacks to do that kneeling-jumping dance after breakfast for our entertainment?" She did a little promo of her concept, knee-bending low then jumping up a couple of times.

He barked a laugh, then stopped. He hadn't done something like that in so long. Since, well, since his mom died. Not much had amused him. His father had seen to that. But this woman with her smart mouth and snark made him want to laugh more often.

She rolled her eyes. "Then there's the bowing. Geezus. You'd think they'd have this flat spot on their forehead for as quick as they did it and as low as they have to go."

He chuckled since he'd thought the same thing many a time. "Demon social strata is still very formal. It's not that much different than Regency England or feudal Russia, so a good comparison."

She sat on the edge of the bed, bouncing a bit, face lit with amusement. "And what the hell was up with the food thing? I thought Surgat was going to pass out when you said I would dine with you."

Lily on the bed. He had to swallow the pictures of her lounging naked on its expanse. *Focus.* "First, no being, other than a true demon, is allowed to dine at Lord Raum's table. Second, my request for food is the ultimate insult. Demons don't eat, they drink." His father's sneering words echoed in his head. The first thing Cal had done after escaping was have a cheeseburger and fries, so the irony of their breakfast pleased him.

She'd stopped bouncing. "You are kidding, right? I'm not a demon, so I am not fit to dine at the table? Because I'm a...pet?" She spat out the last word with nostrils-flared disgust.

He considered her outrage. The cold fire in her eyes, the curl of her lip, the gaze down her nose. "You would be the perfect demon lady. That condescending tone would cut to the bone."

"I'm not acting. That's some Grade-A bullshit right there."

He cracked another laugh. He could definitely get used to this. "Agreed. I didn't demand you eat with me to provoke my father. It *is* bullshit. And I won't have it."

She crossed her arms and considered him down that pert nose. "Okay."

A knock at the door heralded their bags. "May I settle your effects, my Lord, and those of your pet?" The male servant, also a vampire, as would be all servants in a demon household, wouldn't even look into Cal's eyes.

"You may."

Lily shot him an amused side-eye, but said nothing.

"I believe we will tour the Asian Museum of Art this afternoon. It has a lovely collection of pan-Asian exhibits." He pontificated on mythical plans for their 'visit' while the servant worked.

Several minutes later, the male returned. "Your clothing and effects are prepared, my Lord. Do you require anything else?"

"You may leave."

When the door closed, Lily giggled, slapping a hand over her mouth. "Dude. This is gonna be *fun*."

That sobered him. It could be fun, insofar as he was spending time with this wily wolf. Although loath to pour cold water on it, he saw no option. "It could be, but we have a job to do. When I start asking questions about Grigori, about the conspiracy, it could trigger some nasty reactions."

With his words, her amusement flitted away. He already missed the impish grin.

"A job. To hold some Pure Paranormal assholes accountable? Fits in my definition of fun." Her grim visage promised retaliation.

Satisfaction curled through him. His father may believe Clan Sanguis to be the superior race, but Cal would put his bet on the wolf shifter named Moonlight Lily Foster in any battle.

CHAPTER 9

If not for the need for a carefully crafted act, Lily probably would've gone on a rampage by now. The condescension. Their reluctance to fill her water glass after every sip the way they did Cal's. Her blood simmered in her veins. Only after Cal's sharp rebuke had the servants recognized he wouldn't tolerate the poor service.

Even though she should be wolfing down her cheeseburger and fries—petty, but she couldn't resist the plebian request in the face of Surgat's superiority—she had to force the meal down. Not that the food tasted bad, she'd rarely had such savory, juicy burgers.

But the normal undercover butterflies cruising around in her stomach had turned to bees when they came into this palace. Nothing here was normal to her. Starting with her surroundings. She didn't want to touch anything, even look the wrong way, in case she broke something valuable. The tour Cal had given her in the hour between their arrival and breakfast made her want to run screaming from the creepy museum to Italian opulence. Especially with the obsequious vampire servants' heads almost touching the floor as Cal passed. For her, nothing. But he'd made sure she had the layout of the great square building, including where they'd go after they ate.

Would they find someone, even the real Grigori, in his rooms? The one who'd killed those forty humans, stacking them in a room when done like so much trash. Heat built in her stomach. *Down girl.* She was supposed to be a docile, empty-headed little pet for her demon lord's blood needs.

And speaking of demon lord...Cal? How had he joined the Human Paranormal Clan when he clearly belonged in Clan Sanguis? She peeked through her lashes at him as he sipped a ruby red glass of blood wine. She'd detected the substance had been added and declined with a ball of revulsion rising from her stomach. Raw meat from a kill was one thing, fresh blood from the vein...ew. No.

She took a bite from her burger. At least they knew how to prepare food, rather than just a buffet of blood spread out for them. She didn't quite manage to cover her snicker.

"Something amuses you?" Cal said from his position next to her at the head of the long, polished dining table studded with ornate silver candelabra. "Please. Share. This place is depressing and I need a joke."

"When I first met you, I assumed demons could only consume blood. And I had this vision of a scantily clad woman arrayed on a buffet table, offering herself for dinner. You know, like the cow in *The Restaurant At the End of the Universe.*" She slid her face into impassiveness, then lifted her chin, exposing her neck. "My Lord, may I offer a delicious supply of O-positive to you this evening? Or would you prefer B-negative? We also have HP blood on the menu, but that is at market price."

He laughed, one from deep in his belly she'd never heard from him before. "I haven't read that book in so long. Absurd. But amusing—both the book and the idea of a buffet of blood slaves.

No one does that anymore." He took a sip from his glass, observing her over the rim.

"What?" Demons did that in the past? And how had he read Douglas Adams? Then she caught the glint in his eye. "Oh, you're kidding me."

"Yes. But, no. Demons of a certain status could afford the luxury hundreds of years ago, however, the practice has fallen out of favor. Blood is necessary for our survival. We can tolerate physical food, but get nothing from it. Most see eating as déclassé, though." His eyebrow rose with the wry twist of his lips as he gestured to his plate. "I'm sure this is giving Surgat fits."

Still, drinking blood? Yuck. *Or was it all that different?* In wolf form, she bit her prey's neck to sever the spine, like demons sank fangs into their prey's neck. She shivered a little, but didn't want to examine why. And after she killed the rabbit or whatever, the blood tasted good. She lapped it up before setting to the rest of the carcass. Wait. She killed the animal. They didn't have to.

So who was really barbaric in this equation?

She stilled. Geezus. What a prejudiced jerk she'd been. She swallowed her bite of fries along with the lump in her throat.

"You've gone awful quiet over there, Lily-Girl," Cal said softly.

"Don't call me that." Her voice lashed out like a whip crack, overloud in the cavernous room.

Gasps from the servants echoed behind her.

Oh no. If he only he hadn't called her the nickname Hetty used. She scrambled to find a way to repair the fuck-up in her—and his—cover.

He studied her for a moment, before he said, "My apologies. 'Girl' probably wasn't the right word. Because you certainly aren't that." His gaze swept down to her breasts then back up with a carnal smile, but the set of his jaw spoke of his tension.

What am I? A pet or piece of meat? She gritted her teeth against the snarl threatening. Then her preservation side stepped in. *Stop.* She was playing a part and crossed the line.

With a demon lord in front of his servants.

She cursed her hasty mouth, quickly pasted on a contrite pout, and reached for Cal's hand where it grasped the crystal wine stem. "My Lord—Calum—my apologies. Someone once called me that and I dislike the pet name. I must be tired from the travel." She fluttered her eyelashes. "Let me make it up to you. Please?"

Irritation remained in his expression for a moment before his hand relaxed. "Of course my dear, but you're going to have to be extra nice to me. Do you have any ideas on how you can accomplish that?" He caught and held her gaze with an imperious raised eyebrow.

Who knew the controlled NACS Director could become a demon lord so well?

Sliding back her chair, she sauntered the few steps to him. The subtle flare of his nostrils gave her hips an extra wiggle until she propped her butt on the edge of the table, her left hip brushing his arm. Where had this minx come from? The knowledge she could stop and walk away from this contract at any time? For all her bravado, she'd never been the pick 'em up, fuck 'em, and walk away type. The acting job freed a part of her she didn't release. Ever.

"Shall I make some suggestions?" She dipped her voice seductively. "You can tell me if you approve?"

His lids lowered. Maybe he felt the attraction too. No. Only a good actor. She bent at the waist, deliberately giving the servants watching/not watching a show. She held for a fraction of a second, then said in words only he would hear, lips close enough to brush the edge of his ear, "I think you should sleep on the sofa tonight. Because those beds in NACS quarters are worse than sleeping on the ground." Pasting on an angelic smile, she pulled back enough to take in his face. "What do you think about that?"

The swift intake of breath through his nose moments earlier may have indicated passion. But when she'd straightened, the tiniest bit of humor in his eyes said otherwise. He shoved his chair back, rose swiftly, then swept her up in his arms. "I believe that may be satisfactory. In fact, I believe we will not be bothered for the rest of the day."

For a moment, she'd been a little thrilled to be lifted like that. But this eventual scenario had been prearranged to get the servants to believe they were retiring for the day and wouldn't need anything but each other. She wrapped her arms around his nape and buried her face in the curve of his throat, steeling herself against his scent and the way it made her blood sing through her veins and heat blossom between her legs.

He carried her without effort, all the way to their room, with long strides, as if all too eager for her to make good on the suggestions she'd supposedly whispered. She'd planned the words, the suggestive tone, the sexy half-lidded gaze. But she'd chickened out. Yep. Like the lowliest in the roost, scared of her own shadow and reverted to her fallback, snark.

Better that way. And that whole dream last night? An aberration. Something batteries could alleviate, right?

Images of last night's erotic visions slide-showed in her mind. Him taking her nipples in his mouth, nipping, sucking until she moaned then called his name. The desire flaring in his eyes as he tasted her need. Him poised above her, cock magnificent and glistening with pre-cum, ready to slide his length into her. *Oh my faithless ancestors. Even I can smell my arousal.* She resisted the urge to squirm in his arms.

Her wolf chuffed a laugh. *You want him, bad.*

Don't get your hopes up, girl. This is all an act. He would not want me. A packless mercenary bent on finding Pure Paranormal assholes who deserve to die? Mister By The Book would never have me, even if I wanted him too.

Her wolf sat, thick tail curled around her front paws and cocked her head to the side. *I want him.*

You...

For mine.

*But...*Then it sank in. Her wolf *wanted* him.

As her mate.

She stiffened. *No.*

"Whoa. Calm down, my love. We're almost there." Cal shifted her in his arms, finished taking the last stair to the second floor.

Her wolf started panting a little, revealing her smile. And her wicked canines.

You wouldn't. He's a demon, not a shifter.

Her wolf stood and shook. *Little ago you didn't think demons so bad. Didn't last night either. Doesn't matter. Too late.* She turned and headed for the door. *I go to closet.*

This is not fair!

The door slammed behind her wolf, but not before the canine barked a laugh.

"Lily?" Cal said.

"What?" she snapped. She looked up at him, his strong jaw and chiseled cheekbones. Nose that had been broken a couple of times. How had that not healed back properly? He was a demon. Her demon.

No. A demon her wolf wanted.

"I said, could you get the door handle. Please?"

"Oh. Yes." She glanced over her shoulder to the doors, the snake offering Eve the apple at her eye level. Apropos. She reached down and depressed the lever as Cal pushed with his shoulder. One side swung wide and he maneuvered through.

He kicked the door shut with his heel. The carved panel swung out of sight. She did a double-take. Did that snake wink at her?

"Good job," Cal said. "Close enough to how we planned. Now

we just have to wait a bit and we'll be able to sneak out." He took more paces into the room.

Still carrying her.

She couldn't be in his arms right now. Even if her wolf wanted him. She crossed her arms as Chip rushed to the forefront. With a surly tone, she said, "You can put me down."

He blinked, and said with utmost care, "Yes, I can."

She unwound her arms and leveled him her most evil glare. "Put me down. Now."

"Sure." His supporting arms fell away.

She screeched, bracing for impact on the hard, carpet-covered stone.

And landed on the sofa. Which wasn't nearly as soft as she would've hoped, but a hell of a lot more cushy than the floor. She used the single bounce to bound to her feet. "What in the hell?"

"You appeared to want to be out of my arms as quickly as possible." A muscle jumped in his cheek. "I obliged."

Two steps later, she stood toe-to-toe with him. Reached up to poke her finger inches from his nose. "You are an asshole."

He leaned down, frustration written in the frown locking his brows. "You're an asshole, too."

Her gaze had zeroed in on his lips, before she ripped them away. Dammit. He was right. No backing down, though. "You didn't have to hold me for so long." The words came out far lower and huskier than intended.

Heat flared in his eyes. His hands came up to grasp her upper arms. Not hard, but loose enough to pull away should she want. Did she want?

The wolf side of her said 'Closer' between pants. The other side tried to push the sneaky canine back in the closet. Lily's breathing accelerated.

Oh yes, she wanted. Her lips were so dry and she darted her

tongue out to moisten them, wanting, hungering for his kiss. Should she initiate—

He bent his head to close the distance and his lips settled on hers.

Oh, yasss...

CHAPTER 10

Lily clutched his shirt and pulled Cal closer, hands moving to tunnel into his hair.

His body hardened against her softness. Holy Gods. He licked along the seam of her lips, then swept in, exploring, stroking, stoking the need in him. His hand swept to her ass, kneading as he hauled her hips against his. Skin. His fingers skated under the silky top, skimming up her back.

With a soft moan she pressed her body closer, the carnal kiss, the peaked points of her breasts, and the scratch of her nails against his scalp drove him mad.

So long since... More. Gods he needed more. Hungry to make her as wild as the need pulsing in him, his fingers glided up her ribcage. Brushed the silk of her bra. Thumb found the nipple, already tight. Rubbed. Back and forth. Around. Circling.

The nub pebbled. Her head fell back, and she arched, offering her breasts to him, her body to him.

The smooth, exposed column of her neck caught his attention, the pulse beating frantic against the fragile skin. The scent of her blood surrounded him, called a siren's song, luring him, begging him to taste her as he sunk his cock into her.

His fangs descended, their razor-sharp tips ready to bring him the promised ecstasy.

Fangs. He froze as horror clawed through him. Frigid water wouldn't have brought him back to reality faster from what he'd been about to do.

Take blood from Lily without her consent.

"Lily," he husked as he tried to bring his breathing back under control. He brought her gently back to standing, instead of pressed against his groin, grinding her hips against the exquisitely painful length of his cock.

The haze of desire cleared in her hooded eyes and she licked her lips. "What?"

The words didn't want to form, but he forced them. "We can't do this." He grasped for any excuse he could find. Her boss. He was still her boss. "It won't happen again. You can make a complaint with HR when we return to the Rock."

Several steps back gave her distance. She composed herself. Straightened her top and swept her hair back with jerky motions. "Don't worry. I'm not going to make a report." Her tone emerged strangled.

He gathered the composed director mantle around him. "What I did was completely wrong. As your superior—"

She swung back to face him, a snarl on her lip. "You are *not* my superior." Her words would've frightened a wolf from his kill.

"Your superior on paper." He sliced his hand through the air. "I'm the Director of NACS. You are my employee. I'm not supposed to be kissing my employee."

She snorted a laugh. "You didn't just *kiss* me. And what rule says you shouldn't?"

"It's not important which rule applies. It's there." He scrubbed a hand through his hair. Stubborn shifter. "And I can't believe I'm practically begging you to file a complaint against me."

"It'd be a black eye, eh?"

"Yes."

She crossed her arms, one slim brow arched. "You didn't do anything I didn't want to participate in. I wasn't asking, nor did you promise, any benefit from having sex with you, including employment. I am a contractor. Ergo, not a NAC Form 2004 employee, and not subject to the sexual harassment rule, Section 5, 2-point-oh 5."

The rule? She knew the provisions and the sections?

"You thought I wouldn't read the manual?" She tilted her head to the side and curled her lip. "Whatever happened between us wasn't sexual harassment."

If she had a problem with blood sucking, this would warn her off. "Fine. I was about to sink my fangs into you. I thought you might object. Is that enough reason?"

Color drained from her face. "You were going to bite me?"

"Keep it down." He crossed his arms. "Of course I was going to bite you. I'm a demon. It's what we like to do."

A flush rose to her face. "No biting."

"Like I said, this won't happen again." She made an attempt to speak, but he plowed on. "It's a quarter after ten. We've got about fifteen minutes until we need to get going. We should get some work done before Raum returns. I didn't know if you wanted to change before we left."

For a moment she remained silent, as if debating within herself. Finally, she said, "I'll change."

Hunger slammed back into him as he tracked the sway of her hips before she disappeared into the bathroom. The door *snicked* shut with finality.

He swiped a hand over his face. The little shifter presented nothing but trouble. *Damn hot trouble.* Shit. Not during an investigation. And she'd made it clear she wouldn't condone biting. Anything with her couldn't work. Taking of blood was part of the demon sexual relationship.

As if to clear his thoughts, he shook his head. Yet her image, head thrown back, surrendering to him, wouldn't be erased. Gods dammit. The mission. Focus on the fucking mission.

The bathroom door opened to reveal a very different Lily. Gone was the sexy, purple-booted siren, replaced by a sporty version of a starlet ready for a little breaking and entering. She'd braided her hair, but coiled the length around her head in a coronet, wisps fanning her forehead, making her green-gold eyes appear even more huge. Black jeans skimmed her legs, a black silky blouse, then a light black jacket. Flat black tennis shoes completed the outfit.

She carried an extra set of clothing and stuffed the items in her small backpack. The leather bag already contained a couple of pistols with extra magazines in a hidden back pocket normally used for electronic equipment. Preparation. He liked that in a female. Correction. He liked that in an employee.

Speaking of preparation, the blazer had to go. He went to the closet located at the entrance to the bathroom, shrugged out of the restrictive garment, and donned a light black jacket to conceal the gun he carried at the small of his back. Not that anyone around here would challenge him if they saw the automatic pistol. Being armed in the demon community came as a given.

She crossed her arms and challenged, "You ready?"

He flipped his wrist and glanced at his watch. "Been ready now for fourteen minutes."

The barest hint of a smile flitted across her face. "Then let's do this." She marched to the door leading to the courtyard's gallery.

For some reason he didn't want to explore, the sight of her smile made him happy. For the love of the Gods. He needed to get his mind on the job. "Not that way. Come on." He crossed to the tapestry on the far wall, pushed aside the heavy fabric, and placed his palm on a small mar in the plaster. The words came to his mind and he chanted the spell.

The smooth, white surface dissolved and a narrow doorway appeared.

"Figures this creepy house would have secret passages," she murmured.

He suppressed his grin. Creepy fit this mausoleum, a building housing the ghosts of his father's cruel actions and ambitions. "Come on. Quietly now."

She passed through the opening, allowing the heavy fabric to settle in place.

Best to close it, in case Surgat comes in," he whispered. The scant light disappeared as the entrance rematerialized.

"I'm going to slide around you, since we need to go that way."

She flattened herself against the cool stone wall as he eased by, chest to chest, pelvis to pelvis. *Oh shit.* He sucked a breath. His body's reaction to the contact said all of his pitiful protestations were moot. The way every nerve ending in him started firing at her mere touch, this wasn't a casual attraction.

Not now. Focus on the mission. "Do you need a light?"

"No. I can see well enough. How do you know these exist?"

He started down the passage, turned the corner, continued down a flight of rough stairs. "I grew up here. Raum is my father."

CHAPTER 11

Oh hell. Lily reined in her shout to a stage whisper. "Lord Raum is your father?"

"He's the DNA donor only." His calm tone belayed the tension she sensed thrumming in his muscles.

Even worse. Grigori was his brother. Holy guacamole.

"He's my half-brother. Technically." He'd muttered the last words.

Anger zipped through her, eliminating her shock. "You did not just read my mind."

"No. Your defenses are fine." He stopped after the last stair, turning to her. "I'll give you the whole twisted family tree later." He didn't wait for her answer, but pivoted and continued down the passage, taking a left at a crossroads, with her trailing behind.

She followed him up another flight of stairs, a left, then maybe thirty yards into the passage, he stopped and faced the wall. Nothing appeared out of the ordinary in the stone's pattern, like when Cal made the wall reappear minutes ago. *Don't use your eyes, gal. That's what your nose is for.*

Shoving the lid open a fraction did the trick. The essence of the demon next to her flooded in, but she shoved the delicious scent aside. The other odors were the same, but not. Demon, like Cal, but different from each other in their basic makeup. What they wore. Who they fed from. But most of them were old and faded. Nothing new but she and Cal in this place for maybe months.

Yet, something different lay beyond the wall. She placed her backpack on the floor without a sound, dissecting the scents. Vampires had been here, like Surgat—she picked up the lingering odors of his anxiety. But one in specific was stronger than others. It should be his brother.

"You ready?"

"Nose is open," she whispered back. Her muscles tensed. What would he find? His brother? Or no one at all? She tossed off the lid to her nose. Better to let it get swamped than not enough information.

Cal put his hand on her shoulder, then his words dissolved the wall.

Air rushed into the passage, the overwhelming reek of his demon brother assaulted her and she had to shove it aside. She listened for a moment, her enhanced hearing picked up the whoosh of breathing and the heartbeat of one body. She held up her index finger.

He nodded his understanding the gesture meant 'one being', then squeezed her shoulder three times, the third being the standard security training signal to move in. He tossed aside the fabric covering the entry, and took silent steps into the chamber.

Only a couple of levels above the intense darkness of the secret passage, her eyes easily adjusted to the light. The tapestry fell back into place covering their exit and she readied herself as best as possible.

The demon's essence swamped her nose. The smoky scent. The...*What was that*?

A demon, the spitting image of the one who had exploded in

the NACS morgue sat up in the bed where he'd been lounging and staring at a laptop. He eyed them, then his lips twisted into the semblance of a smile. He put the computer aside and stood.

Naked.

Great. She'd seen Grigori naked for a fraction of a second. Same tanned skin, broad shoulders and perfect, blonde visage. She inched to the side as he approached Cal. With distance she'd have a better chance if the fake Grigori chose to attack.

Cal remained still, neither making a move to welcome, nor one to repel. Instead, he widened his stance a bit and kept his hands free to move. When Grigori stopped a couple of feet from him, Cal said, "Brother. I was told we couldn't visit you, but I thought since you were always a practitioner of rule-breaking, you would appreciate Lily and me coming by."

Civilized. More than she'd be able to achieve. 'Hi asshole, who are you?' would be more her line of questioning.

Grigori tossed his head back and laughed. He held his arms out and started forward as if to hug, a wide smile warming his face. "My brother is always a welcome sight."

The scent she'd been trying to isolate came to her. She sprung toward them with no time to shift. "Fae!"

Cal spun, narrowly avoiding the wicked, double-edged long knife which had appeared in the imposter's hand.

Lily landed on the fae's back, one arm under his chin. The other she hooked at his elbow, restricting movement of his knife hand.

Fake-Grigori's other hand tore at her arm banding his neck, but she'd gotten her elbow at his Adam's apple and started squeezing.

Great Wolf, but he is strong.

He danced and shifted wildly, trying to keep his back and her to Cal. Already he'd begun to weaken, his motions slowing. He shifted the knife to his free hand.

Shit. She gritted her teeth on a snarl as he raised the knife intending to stab the arm which steadily cut off the supply of blood to his brain.

His motion a blur, he stabbed backward toward her arm.

He hadn't counted on her natural predator's reaction speed, faster than a fae. She raked that arm up, lifting his chin. Along with the gurgle from where the blade embedded in his windpipe, a white-hot pain shot up her arm, and she clenched her teeth against it. *Don't you fucking let go.*

Under her, the fae's muscles began to slacken.

Yes! She leapt free as he fell to his knees, and she circled, holding her left arm above the elbow where the knife's edge slid by. By her faithless ancestors, that one burned with the flame of a dragon. She hated knife wounds. Shooting was preferable.

She snuck a glance to Cal, who stared at the elf. Right. Best keep an eye on the threat.

The impostor lay gasping on the ground, the wide blade where he'd stabbed himself buried more than half its length deep directly into the right side of his neck, emerging on the left. Bright crimson fae blood glinting with gold bubbled from the entry and exit. By the amount, he'd hit something important. His features began to morph. Elf-blue eyes. Silver-blond hair in a long intricate braid. And it clicked—fae silver comprised the blade.

Bastard. The wound in her arm would take forever to heal. She clamped down even harder with her hand.

He reached for something, near the fireplace and desk.

"Cal!"

Cal stepped on the elf's hand. "Can't have you calling your gold." It would allow the impostor to conjure a vortex and disappear to who knows where. "We need to have a chat, elf."

Chat? She snorted a short laugh. "I'm not sure he'll be able to answer questions. He has a small problem embedded in his windpipe."

"Sure he can." Cal stooped down and managed to gain control of the elf's hands, covering them with his. His intent expression could be chiseled from stone by one of the great masters. Then he took a deep breath.

"What are you doing?" A wave of mental energy blasted her. She staggered to the side, shoulder slamming into an armoire. Bile rose and she gagged, but forced it back down. What in the hell? She turned back to Cal, ready to defend against whatever had attacked.

But he'd somehow remained in his position, kneeling next to the elf, whose eyes had rolled into the back of his head.

Protect his back. She scanned for the threat. Nothing. No sound, no new smell. That meant it had come from...

Cal.

CHAPTER 12

He wished he could've warned Lily, but it would've alerted the impostor. The elf's mental defenses had been strong, maybe even aided by a spell.

No matter.

Nothing could withstand Cal when he chose to enter via shock and awe.

Like a tank, he climbed over the crushed remains of the barrier until he had full access. He swatted aside the impostor's fear and hatred. Ignored the scenes from memories floating by.

Who do you receive your orders from?

The elf hastily tried to throw up blocks.

Cal hit him again with the energy, this time focused in a narrow beam, targeted at the unprotected psyche, instead of a system of walls.

The elf's scream bubbled in his throat.

Tell me. I may let you live.

No. They'll kill me. You kill me. Now.

Tell me and I'll do it.

No. Some of the fake-Grigori's natural arrogance rose to the surface.

Then I'll take it. He gathered his psychic powers, preparing to blast him again.

No! I...I report to Lord Raum.

Gods dammit. He knew it. That sonofabitch had gone too far. Cal sucked back his fury. Wait. It couldn't be just his father. No fae would willingly report to a demon. He regathered his energy, narrowed it like a laser to project his next words at the level of a bullhorn. *Bullshit. Who do you report to?*

The reverberations echoed through the elf's psyche, turning it into a quivering mess for several moments. *Zack*, he finally admitted. An image floated by and Cal committed the face to his own memory. It matched the Clan Fae Council Representative.

The elf's psyche curled itself into a small ball as far back in his mind as possible, cowering. Cal projected himself in and strode over, picked the huddled ball up by the scruff of its neck. He grasped the imposter's name from the echoes in the fae's mind. *What will it be, Tyron? Transportation to Enchanted Rock for trial, or I do what you asked earlier?*

Tyron hung limp as a wet plastic bag. *You...You do it.*

Very well.

Not like Cal had much choice. Where would he store the fae until he and Lily could transport him for trial? Cal removed himself from elf's mind, wishing he could take a shower. The images of death and torture he'd seen committed by Tyron made him wish he could kill the bastard a hundred times. He grasped the hilt and pulled the long knife free from the male's neck, hefting it in his palm. Nice. Shimmering red-gold blood poured from the elf's wounds, doubling the large puddle already formed in a matter of seconds. But that in itself wouldn't be fatal. Elves were tough assholes to kill. Only two ways Cal knew—dragon fire or cutting off their heads. And he had the manner in hand. He raised the long knife like a sword. His hand descended.

"Cal, what are you doing?" Lily's strained voice rose.

Her question didn't halt the fae silver blade, which made the termination short work with one stroke. Tyron's head lolled to the side as the shimmering red-gold drained his life away.

Cal dropped the knife next to the body with disgust. "We can't take him with us and he asked to be ended."

For a moment she gaped at him. "So that *was* you with the psychic energy. You knocked me sideways."

"My mother may have bought her way into the clan, but I still had to have something to show. It's what qualified me to enter Clan HP." He didn't have to say he trusted her not to reveal his secret. She had already claimed so many, one more didn't matter much. "I could've warned you, but it might have given him time to reinforce his defenses. Thanks for having my back while I went in. That was one fucked up elf."

Let Surgat find the body and report it to his father. Come this evening and Lord Raum's return, Cal would know how deep his father had sunk. Now, nothing would keep him from exposing the evil demon's corruption.

A familiar scent hit him. Blood. His eyes sought its source. Bright, sweet blood stained Lily's fingers where they covered her arm. Dammit. He rushed to her. "He got you?"

She nodded. "With the knife."

Of fae silver. Like human silver on steroids. A cut wouldn't kill unless it hit her heart, but the injury would hurt like a bite from Cerberius's hell hounds and take forever to heal.

Unless he helped her along.

"I think I have a way to make it better, but—"

"I don't care what you have to do, do it." Her pallor stood testament to her pain. A fine sheen of sweat covered her forehead.

The method would heal her, but she wouldn't like it.

"Okay." He pulled back his cuff as his fangs descended. One of the wickedly sharp tips ripped open a vein at his wrist. Blood welled immediately, starting to run down his arm. He held it to her mouth, which had formed an 'O'. Would she do it? He lifted a corner of his lips in encouragement. "Are you going to heal yourself or just stand there? Drink."

He wanted to urge her with his mind, but he knew that would be a certain path to eradicate her trust forever. Instead, he tried logic as the blood dripped-dripped from his wrist. "You will not turn into a vampire. Since you're a paranormal, my blood will only repair you in a couple of hours, while removing the pain associated with your body's reaction to the knife. It makes sense. Drink." He forced a note of humor in to his tone. "It's dripping on the floor."

She blinked as if only now taking in his words. She wet her lips with her tongue before darting out to swipe a drop.

His gut clenched with the delicate action. He'd half expected her to push back on his offering and was unprepared for the erotic vision.

Surprise flitted across her face a split second before she placed her lips across the wound. Her brows swooped together over lashes fanned against her cheeks. A sigh of contentment gusted from her as she sucked gently, lips light as a feather, tongue a breath of air against his skin.

And that fast, he grew granite-hard. His hips rocked in time with the suction. Fangs burst forward, begged to taste the blood pulsing under the soft skin of her neck. Her pressure increased, erotic and primal. Desire began to short-circuit his mind. She had to cease, or he couldn't control his demon. "You can stop," he said, proud of the lack of panic in his voice.

Instead, she brought her hands up to hold his wrist in place, demanding more.

His fangs descended as his demon came forward. He yanked his arm away from her mouth.

She stumbled forward, but caught herself. The confusion clouding her eyes faded to shock. "Did I...did I just..."

He sealed up the wound on his wrist with his tongue, the special proteins in his saliva making short work of the open skin. "Yes, you did." *And it fucking rocked my world.* As a special torture, his groin muscles contracted, a pale, desperate attempt to capture the orgasm his body craved right now. He bit back a groan. "You have some blood on your chin," he choked out. She did, but he'd say anything right now to distract her from his lack of composure.

She swiped at it with her finger, then brought it to her mouth, slid it past her lips. "Mmm." She pulled it out slowly, as if it had been the most delicious thing she'd ever tasted. As if she had no idea how her words would affect him, she said. "I never realized demon blood would taste so good. You're like...chocolate. Dark, a little bitter. Godiva would pay good money for that."

The words punched him in the gut.

No one had told him that before. None of the NACS officers he'd worked with and had to field-medic with his blood said anything about the taste. Granted, they'd all been out cold, so they couldn't have known he donated Clan Sanguis blood, they believed they'd been healed faster by the med ward. And none of the short, miserable attempts at relationships had ever wanted to sample his blood, let alone tell him he tasted better than gourmet chocolate.

His gaze narrowed in on her hand. The question burst from him before he could rein it back. "May I taste you?"

"What?"

"Your fingers. They still have the blood from your wound. My I taste it?"

For a moment, she made no response. Just when he believed she'd snap to and deliver a snarky reply, she lifted her hand, holding it to him, a slight tremble in the fingers.

His mouth dried at her offer. *Do it before she changes her mind.* He grasped her hand lightly, as if a courtier, and brought it toward him. His lips found her life essence and swiped at a patch of the bright crimson on her knuckle. Light, delicate. Intoxicating. More. He needed more of her.

His fangs came forward once again and he struggled to release her hand before he hauled her into his arms and feasted at her neck. "You taste amazing," he choked out.

The soft smile that graced her face almost undid him. "Thank you."

Wait. A small voice piped up in the back of his mind. *Doesn't that mean something?* No shifter blood should taste like this. Like he would crave her taste for eternity.

Oh Fuck. *Don't say it.*

But, she could be your mate-

No. She can't be, he snarled.

"Cal?'

He shook himself free of his thoughts. "Planning what we need to do next."

"Looks like I've stopped bleeding. And call me crazy, but the pain is negligible." She held up her arm as evidence, then enveloped him in a hug. "I knew Clan Sanguis blood was powerful, but I had no idea it could heal like this."

Denial froze him in place. It shouldn't be working so fast. It would only do that because...

His blood recognized her. Healed her as it would him. It rarely happened. One in hundreds of demons ever found the connection. Lily was *his*.

She released him then stood back, poking a finger at the slit in her jacket, then she let her arm fall. "I don't think you can see the cut, can you?" She turned quizzical eyes to him. "Are you okay?"

About as far away from okay as any demon could be. *Act normal, idiot.* "I'm fine. I don't notice the cut, but I can smell your blood. Others might. We're kind of programmed for it. Since we still have more to do, I'd suggest you change into what you brought."

"Gah. I get it." She made for the tapestry.

No, she didn't get it at all. Her essence filled him, clogged his brain with inappropriate thoughts—simultaneously needing to stomp that elf into dust for harming her and hungering to sink deep into her with both cock and fang. These urges had to stop. He needed to be in the here and now for his job and for his mate's safety.

Gods dammit. The idea had already gained traction and would not be removed. This would be painful. Finding, then denying your mate. The ultimate torture of a demon. So few received the call. Then, if the King denied the union in lieu of another... But that particular form of torture was for acknowledged members of the clan. As an HP, not Clan Sanguis, King Krian couldn't force Cal's union with anyone. He could 'union' with her all he wanted.

And that set off another round of forcing fangs back and talking himself out of taking a sip, a little tiny one. *Do your damn job, Stavros.* "I'll see if there's anything here we can get intel from," he announced.

Lily materialized at his side as he finished his sweep of the bathroom and chamber. She'd chosen black again, a jeans jacket and low-contrast graphic t-shirt. If not for her pale skin and flashing gold eyes, she could still blend into the night. And her blood no longer scented the air freely, thank the Gods.

"Other than the laptop, I didn't see anything. Can you check?" Maybe she could sniff out some magic or hidden compartment he hadn't found.

Running the perimeter, she started at the door, taking her time to suss out scents.

He leaned a shoulder against the cool plaster wall. "How did you know it wasn't my brother?"

She lifted her nose from a chest of drawers. "I smelled the fae on him." She cocked her head. "You moved out of the way of his knife pretty quick. You knew he wasn't your brother too."

He crossed his arms at his chest. "That asshole would never have been glad to see me."

"Sibling love," she said, her tone drier than the Gobi Desert. The nose went back to action over an antique desk next to the fireplace.

Yeah. Sibling love. Something he'd never shared with Grigori. Little brother had made sure to make Cal's life a living hell. His fingers crept to the bridge of his nose, and fought down the rage at the memory of how it came to be crooked, when everyone knew demons healed perfectly. Not when cut with a fae blade. It had taken Cal months to mend, since Grigori and his sycophants ensured it got ripped open almost every day. And his father couldn't have cared less. 'That's what demon males do.' No. That's what sociopathic demon males do. Seeing his brother on the morgue's table hadn't sparked any sympathy or familial feelings. The world was better for Grigori not being in it.

"I think I have something." Lily stood before the open drawer of the desk. She held her right elbow in her left hand, finger tapping her lips, eyes narrowed.

He straightened and crossed the short distance. A peek into the drawer revealed simple stationary items, including an expensive gold pen bearing Raum's crest, all neatly placed.

"Fae gold." she said, tone pensive. "It could be what he was calling to create a portal."

Dammit. He hadn't thought of the pen when he'd search the desk earlier as it appeared to be the same as every other pen Cal had encountered in Raum's household. "We'll take it."

"I think it's a bad idea. There's a whiff of ozone and licorice attached to it, what I've come to associate with Clan Magic." Her brow cleared. "I have an idea." She sprinted to the bathroom and returned with a hand towel. "I'll pick it up with this."

"No. Let me do it." He reached for the terrycloth.

She yanked the towel away and stepped between him and the

drawer, cloth behind her back. "No. If the shit hits the fan, you'd be best to hang around to get help."

All of his demon instincts screamed she shouldn't take the chance. What if mere removal would trigger whatever magic the pen carried? Logic dictated otherwise.

"Fine." He stepped away. "But check the rest of the room first. If you're going to get blown to bits or teleported to Gods know where, we could at least be sure you'd found everything before I had to come save your ass." He deadpanned his tone.

Her stare and gaping mouth made him believe she hadn't gotten his humor. Then her lips began to shift, until a blinding smile replaced the shocked oval. She punched him in the arm. "Damn, Stavros. I'm beginning to think you might have a sense of humor after all. *My* sense of humor." She continued her examination, finishing the rest of the chamber and the bathroom in short order.

"You might want to stand in the passage, maybe even wall it back up," she said. "I'm hoping the towel proves enough a barrier, but..." She shrugged and turned toward the drawer.

He clamped a hand on her shoulder. "If you're teleported somewhere, I'm coming with you. No arguments." And if she got blown to bits, he'd have it on his conscience. For about point-oh-oh-one seconds.

The mulish push of her jaw indicated she didn't agree with his decision, but she reached for the pen.

Every muscle in his body locked, preparing for the worst. Because if Lily wasn't in this world, it would, indeed, be the worst.

CHAPTER 13

After the fuckery this group had been committing, Lily wouldn't put anything past them. Merely moving the fae gold pen could trigger an adverse reaction. She'd wrapped the towel around her right hand. No contact with her skin. Possibly, the slim tube shouldn't be moved at all. But the pen couldn't be left behind in case information could be gleaned.

Cal's hand on her shoulder radiated tension.

Not helpful she wanted to sing-song. But she understood his wariness of being separated. Staying with your partner was a good idea as long as both didn't go down. But if they got sucked somewhere together, they would be better off, statistically. Hopefully. *Enough overthinking. Get it over with.*

Lily hauled in a breath and steadied her hand. She closed it around the pen.

No reaction. She said a little prayer of thanks to the Great Wolf. Now to remove it. With infinite care, she pulled her hand up with the pen enclosed in the thick terrycloth barrier.

Her lungs expanded with new air. She hurried to roll the object in the towel, tucking the ends to secure it. Cal's hand had fallen away and she missed the feeling of security the warmth represented.

She stilled. Now she relied on him to feel secure? *Get a grip, woman.*

"What?" Cal said, urgency flaring in his voice.

"Nothing." Dammit. She picked up her purse-backpack from the floor near the tapestry where she'd left the bag after changing, slid a side zipper open, and stashed the towel-wrapped bundle inside. She slung the bag over her shoulder. "I folded the jacket and shirt with the blood in the middle, then rolled the bundle up tight. *I* can still smell the blood, but I didn't know if you can. If you want, we can ditch it."

He inhaled, a strange look crossing his features. "No. I think we're good for now. Ready?"

She stepped beyond him into the passage, hefting the backpack. At least they were one for two. After he'd sealed the breach, she asked, "Where are we going?" She'd whispered her question while their eyes adjusted to the dark.

"To see an old friend before my father returns," he murmured. "Westryn might have some good intel about what's going on in the Demon Court."

"Why didn't you ask him if Lord Raum was home before we arrived?"

"He's a blood smuggler and like all criminals, information can be bought. His knowledge of my inquiries would be enough to be valuable. I trust him, but it's better not to put him in a bad spot. Besides, by now, Lord Raum knows we're in town. I had hoped to surprise him." Instead of doubling back, he started down the passage in the direction not earlier traveled.

So the NACS Director grew up with gangsters? Some friend. She combed her databanks, but didn't come up with anything matching the name he'd given. This 'Westryn' must keep a profile low enough not to land on Hebert Security's organized crime radar. Or he kept his activity within Clan Sanguis.

It still didn't explain how Cal and he knew each other. She suppressed a short snort. Not that she should be surprised. Lord Raum, Cal's father? The demon lord's reputation for cruelty was legendary. What had Cal's childhood been like? A cruel father, Grigori his brother. It couldn't have been a happy life with those two. By the Great Wolf. She'd have loved a crack at that Grigori. Forty humans he murdered without care. Too bad he couldn't die twice.

Cal stopped at a corner. "Is that growling coming from you?"

Shit. "Yeah. Bad thoughts."

"Get them all the time, but you might want to keep it down, or Hades may wonder if he'd misplaced a hell-hound."

She stifled a laugh. "Thanks. I don't know if I've ever gotten a compliment that nice."

His grin flashed in the gloom. "You're welcome. Come on."

Another smile? She smothered a crack about being careful because he might get used to them. Down more stairs, then a dead end. "There will be guards above us. Cameras, I'm sure. Maybe forty feet on the walls. Follow me exactly. The path gets narrow."

Great. At least the flexible sole of her tennis shoes should limit the sound of her footfalls.

More of the language, a chanted phrase he'd used twice already tonight, and damp, misty air swept in to replace the cold, stale atmosphere of the passage. A weak light filtered in. Fog swirled, reaching into the corridor. He listened and she joined him at the entry. After several moments he tapped her shoulder and gave her a thumbs up. He button-hooked around the corner and she performed the same smooth operation around the other. A murmured phrase barely audible to her ear closed the passage.

He cocked his head to his left and she followed him along the narrow path. Nothing grew against the towering walls, they'd allowed only dirt. On her right, a drop-off. She didn't look for the bottom. Instead, she kept her eyes trained on Cal's back.

A hundred feet or so later, he turned right, away from the compound. The footing had turned from dirt to rock. She didn't dare gaze down as she traversed the narrow strip of granite, maybe about a foot wide. Below them, nothing but mist. Ten steps later—not that she counted—she reached gratefully for Cal's outstretched hand to bring her safely to the flat space where he stood.

"It's a long way down. Glad you stayed close." His words emerged on a breath close to her.

She shivered. From the drama of his words or the effect of his breath tickling her ear, she didn't quite know. Or the memory of the taste of his blood? She pushed the idea aside, as she had the idea when they were kissing that it wouldn't be so bad if he had bitten her.

"There's some stairs ahead." He took her hand and tugged her forward. "They're uneven and dangerous, especially with the fog. Watch your step."

Focus. She started down the steep, precarious ledges, each slick with moisture, small pebbles, and sand. Cal had to be part mountain goat the way he confidently made his way down. Her rubber soles were no match for the substrate. She slid, overcompensated, and fell right into his back.

Cal caught her with one arm, saving them both from falling to the boulders below. He set her back on her feet with humor sparkling in his eyes. "You okay?"

"Dangerous? How about treacherous as fuck," she muttered between gasps for air.

"It's easier going up. Ready?"

"Born ready."

"I can tell."

For a moment her heart slammed hard against her ribs. The

tenderness in his tone, the way his thumbs stroked her upper arms, nearly undid her. He searched her eyes as if he could see into her soul. Insecurity welled. No male had ever looked at her like this, like she was more than a runt and mattered beyond her nose's ability. "Shouldn't we be going?"

He blinked. Then without a word, he turned and started down the so-called stairs.

A pit formed in her stomach with the loss of his warm hand and regard. She shoved aside the emptiness. Better this way.

Careful foot after careful foot, she navigated through the dense fog. She stepped on firm ground in a cavern and sent a quick prayer of thanks to the Great Wolf. To her left, the dome soared overhead easily at least fifty feet, maybe a football field long. Natural or cut by demons, she couldn't tell. Packed sand ground made for easy walking. It held no illumination itself, but lights glowed from a huge square cut into the stone to her right about twenty paces. On the far side from the light sat a jumble of equipment and furniture.

"How often did you come this way?" She kept her voice low.

"As often as I could." The grim words held no humor.

"We're directly under your father's castle, aren't we?"

A low derisive laugh came from Cal. "He'd like that term, castle. Yes. He made this cave but has no idea I know of it. He used it to make his money and fund his rise to power. Killed all who were involved." He nodded toward the light. "This way."

She passed through the square in the rock. By the holes spanning a foot in diameter, she suspected there once had been a great door bolted here. The large square quickly narrowed down to half its size, still big enough to drive a tractor trailer through, then split into three tunnels of unequal size. Cal chose the left passage, the smallest. It narrowed here, maybe three people could walk shoulder-to-shoulder. Fae lights lined the walls and they shimmered on as Cal and she approached. No stacked sandstone like the castle's foundations. This warren had been hollowed from the raw rock. A smugglers tunnel, and that cavern would be where he stored his goods. Huh. What would demons smuggle? The furniture came into better view in her mind's eye. What could be smuggled which would need refrigeration equipment and medical beds—

Oh hell.

"He's a blood smuggler."

If it weren't for the sharp inhale of breath, she may never have known for sure she'd hit the mark. "Was," Cal said after a moment. "He gave the business up one hundred and fifty years ago. After he'd bought his title."

Cal had stripped his tone of any emotion. Which meant it ran deep in this topic. She'd figured out that much about him at least.

"Westryn smuggles blood too. Just not the steal-the-human-and-bleed-them-dry type," he said. "More the don't-want-to-pay-outrageous-taxes-to-the-Blood-Authority-type."

Holy shit. No wonder Cal's brother ended up the way he did. By the amount of beds behind her, the forty Grigori killed were peanuts. "Y'all had civil war over humans, didn't you?" The clan had been split between those wanting to ban the importation of unwilling humans as blood slaves, and those who didn't. The latter lost, resulting in the regulation of blood—if a demon needed or wanted blood beyond his or her pet, the supplier received a price set by the realm. Any blood taken in the wild must leave the human alive. To kill a human for their blood meant potential death to the demon or vampire.

"Yep, demons killed each other over humans seven hundred years or so ago."

Five hundred years before Raum shut down his operation. Meaning he ran illegal operations in that cavern. Probably stole humans, maybe HPs like Hetty, and kept them prisoner for their blood. Human Paranormal blood was akin to steroids for demons and vampires. Healed them faster, satisfied them longer.

She unclenched her jaw. "I'm glad you don't like your dad. I hate his guts, and every other part of him. How you came from him is beyond me."

"What do you mean?" His brows raised, as if astonished.

"You're very dedicated to doing the right thing." She peeked at him from the corner of her eye. "Like obsessed."

"Not all the time," he said, his voice strained.

"Okay, so we kissed and it's not exactly in line with your regulations. It doesn't make what I said any less valid."

"Yeah, well, before you put me on a pedestal, remember, I came from the monster on the hill and my half-brother was Grigori."

"Actually, I'm going to modify my statement. I see a bit of him in you. Sounds like you got your drive from him." She ignored his snort of derision. "But I bet you got your goodness and sense of morals from your mother. I mean, if you were really like the other two males in your family, wouldn't you be out attacking humans, stealing their blood, being part of a plot to take over Enchanted Rock?"

For several moments he maintained a silence. But she could almost hear the gears turning in his head as he paced next to her.

A dead end loomed ahead. "Here's the door," Cal said. "Can you hear anything on the other side?"

She sharpened her ears. What could she hear through rock? "Nope."

He said more low-toned words in the language she'd heard earlier with the same results. He grabbed her hand, palm warm and fingers strong. He led her forward and they were outside in the mist again, even more dense at this level. Was this the famous San Francisco marine layer?

He reengaged the spell. "Not long now, maybe five minutes." He waded through knee-high scrub to a short, well-worn dirt path. A couple of minutes later, a trailhead sign drifted into view out of the ghostly mist. He picked up the pace to a light jog, nothing that would make her break a sweat, especially since they were headed downhill. Not a half mile later, he turned left onto a gravel drive.

Cal's stash house.

Tall hedges screened the house from the road. As she approached the SUV, the locks flipped. She crawled in, barely shutting the door before he put it in gear.

"At this time of day, with this fog, it should take about forty-five minutes," he said.

During the ride, he seemed inclined to leave her with her thoughts. Maybe because the fog meant he had to pay more attention. Maybe because he had his own demons running around his head. She almost snorted a laugh, but caught it before it slipped out. Because, the Great Wolf knew, she had her own. And then his 'friend,' who didn't sound like a friend. And his father, who needed a serious life adjustment. Like a permanent one, ending with death.

The trip flew by with her circling worries. Cal pulled off the highway and into a dingy warehouse district with rows upon rows of derelict, corrugated-tin buildings. He turned down between one row, then parked behind a dumpster at the far end.

He pointed straight out the windshield. The fog lightened a bit here. "We're two rows away from West's building. We'll take it slow. There shouldn't be anyone around. Let me know what you detect."

Smart. She reached for the door's handle. Once out, she slung her pack, wrinkling her nose at the ripe scent from the dumpster. She followed him at a quick pace to the first building, head on a swivel, nasal passages open, ears ready. Cal paused at the first row.

She listened past his breathing, the vehicle sounds from the highway. A motor thrummed. No steps, nothing to indicate activity.

"Are you sure he's there?" She nodded her head toward the

rundown building. "I hear a good-sized generator, but no occupation."

"He's here." Cal's words rang with confidence. "What does your nose say?"

The wind blew toward her. Good for scenting. She lifted the lid. Diesel exhaust. Human. No, human blood. "You're probably right."

"Ready?" At her nod, she followed him across the fifty-yard distance to the next warehouse, climbing the stairs to the crumbling concrete loading dock that ran the distance down the side.

He grabbed the handle of a door with a giant padlock chaining it shut. The panel opened easily. Ah, a spell to make it appear locked. A narrow, decrepit hallway led to another door. Not welcoming at all.

As if the dingy gold plaque didn't say 'NO ADMITTANCE' in engraved black letters. He turned the knob and entered. At the hallway's end, a passenger elevator. Nice trap if someone wanted. The scent of blood caressed her nose now. Close. He entered, then jammed his fingers against three buttons at once.

She followed him into the carriage, but damn if the thing hadn't probably skipped the last half century of service certifications. Yay. The squeaking and groaning on the way down didn't improve her confidence.

The doors opened without her being dropped and squished into roadkill. Cal brought her down a long hallway with another door at the end. Its plaque said 'ABSOLUTELY NO FUCKING ADMITTANCE'. She suppressed a snarky chuckle.

Her ears picked up voices beyond the thick panel. More than one. Best practice for a security raid was one-plus-one—at least one more man than your opponents. By that rule, she and Cal were already outnumbered. Yet, it could be a discussion with an employee. A specific scent hit her receptors. A fae had been through here recently.

Dammit.

Video cameras dotted the ends of the hallways. Maybe with sound or not. She put a hand on Cal's jacket and pulled him to her, as if she were kissing him. She smiled saucily, put her forehead to his and murmured, "There's at least two in there. I smelled a fae, but it could've been recent or hours ago."

He dropped his hands to her hips and tugged her to him, then swooped in for a long, wet, kiss, which would've been mind-blowing if she didn't need to keep her head in the game. Then his fingers wove into hers, and his posture relaxed, tension from his shoulders evaporating. They continued on to the door as if she were his girlfriend and belonged there.

He may, but she didn't. She pulled on her wolf, keeping her close to the surface, then slid her arm out of one of the backpack straps so she could ditch it if needed.

You never knew when shit might go south.

CHAPTER 14

Cal depressed the door handle with a small smile. Westryn, Cal's cousin in some distant way, still had the plaques he'd given him years ago as a joke. As almost an afterthought, he let go of the demon's mind who'd been manning the surveillance system. It had been too easy to find him and bust through his pathetic barriers. West needed to find better help.

The panel swung open, revealing West behind his massive steel and glass desk, a giant, bald male, seated in front of him, his back to Cal. Those massive shoulders tensed under the dark gray suit jacket. Each male had a glass of dark amber liquid in front of them.

Irritation creased West's brow for a fraction of a second, which morphed to recognition. "Cal. What are you doing here?" He jumped to his feet from the plush leather chair, gaining his full height of over six-five. Tie gone from his suit, top shirt buttons undone, he resembled a Wall Street exec ready for his thirty-year old scotch at the end of a tough day, not the smuggler Cal knew him to be.

West's calculating gaze shifted to the male sitting in the chair, but returned quickly to Cal. He rounded the desk, one arm already outstretched to herd them out. "I've got a visitor, but I could meet you and your..." His eyes flicked to Lily. "Pet for dinner. Say seven?"

"I'd love to take you up on the offer, but I'm afraid that's not an option." West had stopped Cal from reaching the point he may be able to see exactly who sat in that chair. Like that would happen. Doing business with a fae? The association could have implications for the conspiracy.

"Westryn, you should know by now Director Stavros will not be deterred." The deep voice came from the stranger, surprising Cal. He rose to his full height, topping both demons by a good foot. The dark gray pinstriped, double-breasted suit fit his enormity perfectly. A silk pocket square in blood-red provided the only nod to color. The fae's vertical scar ran down the left side of his face, briefly interrupted by his eyepatch. The disfigurement and his thick neck made him appear more like an over-dressed mafioso henchman. Despite the loose-limbed stance, the fae's shoulders flexed, ready for action. No doubt he could toss Cal through the dark-wood paneled wall like he weighed nothing more than a sack of oranges.

Griffith Jenkins.

The gentle squeeze of Lily's fingers told Cal she'd recognized him too. If she hadn't known him already, she should've seen his wanted poster plastered all over the bulletin boards in NACS. She edged back, giving her and him space to move. Wise lady.

No one really knew what type of fae Jenkins was, though many had speculations. Didn't matter. He shoved his massive hand in every criminal pie on Earth. Not only that, NACS almost nabbed him a couple of weeks ago during an operation to recover Maya Nagashree, the wife of Clan Magic Council Representative Malcolm Sand. Dammit. Cal couldn't afford to bring him in, let alone play mind games. At least not right now. Despite heading one of the most successful criminal organizations known to NACS, there'd been no whiff of Jenkins in the conspiracy threatening the Council. The Priority One investigation took precedence at this point. Cal cursed his luck. The wily fae could slide out unharmed from a sprung bear trap.

Cal hoped West's office would be enough to act as neutral territory. He stuck out his hand. "Jenkins. I'm not here on NACS business. As long as the dealings don't affect the Council, the affairs of the Demon Court are their own."

The massive fae blinked, recovered, then took Cal's hand for the courtesy. "Director." His stony regard didn't waiver.

West stepped into the pause while Cal and the fae held each other's gazes in a dominance stand-off. "Jenkins and I were just finishing our business," West said.

A knock sounded from the other side of the door.

Cal didn't falter, since Jenkins still presented a threat. Lily would have his back.

"And there's my associate to get you back to your concerns, Jenkins. I appreciate your time today, and we will look into your offer." He walked to the door with the massive fae, apparently unconcerned he discussed business, however vague, in front of the NACS Director.

"I'll expect payment in fae gold," Jenkins rumbled.

"It will be so."

The fae exited without another word or a backward glance.

West shut the door, his face devoid of any emotion. Silence reigned for several moments.

Had Cal miscalculated by coming here? He and West still shared a friendship, right? If not, he'd brought Lily into unnecessary danger.

Then West shook his head with a crack of laughter. "For the love of the Gods, Cal. Could you have come at a worse moment?" West moved to the wet bar, which held a selection of alcohol, all excellent vintage. "Whiskey?"

"Sure." Hopefully West had the information he sought. "I'm sure Lily would like a bourbon as well?"

"Please," she said and made her way to the couch opposite from where West poured the drinks. He handed a glass to her with the smile guaranteed to charm the panties off any willing female. Lily didn't immediately fawn, as West probably would expect. Instead, she cocked her head and surveyed him with amused suspicion as she accepted the drink. "Thank you."

"I'm losing my touch." West handed Cal a glass with two knuckles of the rich, amber liquid. Then he retrieved his from the desk and propped his hip on the surface. He lifted the cut-crystal tumbler and drained the remainder in one swallow, the glass' facets winking in the light. "What brought you here today, Cal? It's been a while. Are your blood suppliers not providing like they should? I can get you a special discount."

"My supply is fine. I make it a point to come by every time I'm in town, you know that. But today, I do happen to need your perspective."

West stared at him as a stranger, as if he hadn't spent portions of his demon adolescence with Cal. Through Grigori's attacks. Defending him against others' slurs, for no one would physically attack Lord Raum's son. Cal had no better brother than West. To see him this distant stole a piece from Cal's soul.

Finally, West set his tumbler on the desk and scrubbed a hand over his face. "You're right. It's been a shitshow lately. Every time I turn around, the Court's Blood Authority is nipping at my vein. I had two shipments of HP blood get picked off. The loss won't kill me, but those really hit deep. Don't suppose you know who might be feeding information to them? "

"No idea." Good for the Blood Authority. West could do so much better than smuggling. "If it gets too bad, you could come work for me."

West barked a laugh. "As if NACS would accept a career criminal." The consideration in his gaze gave Cal some hope, however fast it disappeared behind the veil of ennui. West stood, tumbler in hand and crossed to his bar. "So, what is it you and your agent lady-friend here need?"

"Agent?" Lily swirled her drink and swallowed, then cocked an eyebrow.

"If Cal's here for information, he wouldn't bring his girlfriend. Besides, you're not demon." He aimed his next comment at Cal. "Unless you're going for the ultimate punch to the face to your father, of course. And deliberately shunning his marriage arrangement for you." West selected one of the bottles and poured a hefty measure from it.

Anger thrummed through Cal. He'd never honor any marriage contract his father signed. He resisted a glance at Lily to see how she took the news, as well as the desire to plant a fist in his 'friend's' face. "He's told me on multiple occasions his bastard won't be joining the ranks of the demon elite."

West capped the bottle and returned it to its place amongst its peers. "Grigori's damaged goods. Raum's desperate. Enough to float a possible petition to Krian for your recognition. I've heard he hasn't quite forgiven Raum for the death of his sister. The death of his nephew will anger Krian further, maybe enough to kill him."

"Who said Grigoi's dead? Isn't he on house arrest at Raum's estate?" Cal strove to keep his tone casual, when all of his focus narrowed on the man facing him.

"I hear things." His friend motioned with his glass. "*And*, the king has allowed Golmed to hold your father to the marriage contract he signed for Grigori. Raum's considering you as the proposed substitute, though you aren't of royal blood. Otherwise, buying them out of the contract may well bankrupt him."

"Bankrupt?" Not the great Lord Raum. Nothing could make Cal happier.

"You didn't know." West studied the liquor in his glass for a moment, then said, "His business interests have taken a hit lately. The big segment who frowns on taking humans as cattle are giving no quarter. He might've survived his wife's death and the whispers he killed her, but accepting your brother back was one of the stupider things your father could've done. The demon court has largely shunned him, sensing the king's mood."

"Blood always mattered to Raum the most." *Legitimate blood.* And the obsession got him what he deserved.

West swirled the amber liquid in the tumbler. "It will be his undoing. He's had his head up his ass for so long, chasing that brother of yours and trying to fix his messes. His import business is heavily mortgaged. I'm negotiating to buy the loans. Raum Holdings will be Global Realm Imports by the end of the month." The curl of West's lips spoke of his satisfaction.

"What'd he ever do to you?" Despite the question, Cal's satisfaction couldn't be greater at Raum's fall from grace.

"My reasons are my own." His amber eyes rose to Cal's, grim and glittering, the same amber of his whiskey. "He's not a good demon, and I'm happy to be part of his demise."

"I should've ended this long ago." Despite their disparate positions and distant relation, Cal loved the other demon like a brother.

West's smile contained an edge. "You've got too many damn principles to get revenge like that. I don't. Now what is it you needed from me?"

"Who has Raum been dealing with specifically?" Cal almost didn't ask for the information. West's friendship meant more than his father's ultimate fall, but not the survival of the council. "I've got a line on a conspiracy to take over the North American Council. It led me to him."

West's shoulders lifted, "I'm in his business, not his politics." He took a swig and stared off into the distance for a moment. "His businesses have been hemorrhaging cash to a couple of shell companies, which might be payoffs or funding to your conspiracy. I haven't been able to trace them specifically yet, but I can send you what I have."

"Thanks." Cal's gut said these would be clues. If he could isolate the accounts, they may take him to the leader. Maybe Zack. Maybe someone even higher. What if... What if the real head was Kalypso, the Fae Queen? Little information escaped the secretive Fae Realm. As far as most knew, nothing but sunshine and rainbows existed in the fae cloister. Luckily, Simon deVrys, Deputy Director and son of a prominent lord in the Realm's Seelie Court, told him about Kalypso's ruthless rise to power.

"A friend always has your back, right?" A corner of West's lips lifted and Cal pulled his thoughts from his speculations to behold the demon adolescent who'd taken every opportunity to poke at Raum and Grigori. Cal had never understood why. Friendship? Yes. But there was more to West's hatred. Maybe someday West would tell him.

"We've got company," Lily said, tone urgent. She *thunked* her bourbon on the coffee table and jumped to her feet. One of the guns she'd stashed in her backpack appeared in her hand.

Cal set his glass aside as well and pulled his weapon from the holster at the back of his waistband.

Amusement flitted across West's features. "Don't be silly, I'd have--" Shouts came from the other side of the door.

"Shit." West sprinted to his desk, his finger to his ear. He must have a communicator placed inside. "Over here." He put his right hand to the wall behind his desk and part of the wood paneling slid open. Gunshots echoed from the hallway and he reached into his jacket, pulled out his own large-caliber automatic pistol. "Go down, then two rights. You know your way?"

Cal glanced to Lily and she nodded her understanding, as if

she could read his mind. She'd remain and fight if needed. He turned back to his friend. "We can stay and help."

"This one's not your fight." He put his hand on Cal's shoulder and squeezed. "Go."

"Thanks, West. May the Gods bless you." Cal put his hand on the small of Lily's back and urged her into the passage.

As the panel slid shut behind them, West's furious voice echoed through the escape tunnel. "Who the fuck let Lord Raum's men get in here?"

Cal spun, but too late. He couldn't activate the mechanism to reopen the door. Dammit. Had his father returned early to find the fae imposter dead, and had knew where he could find Cal? Or had his father solely reacted to a threat to his financial empire?

Didn't matter. West had stood up more times than Cal could count. Either reason *was* his fight, dammit.

With Raum's resources directed at West, now could be the perfect time for Cal to confront the source.

CHAPTER 15

Lily pounded after Cal, down a flight of stairs, leapt from the fourth riser, and hit the floor running. That West would have an escape route didn't surprise her. If her internal compass proved right, they were headed toward the highway.

From above them, a gun battle erupted, automatic fire heavy. Great Wolf—that had to be a fifty-caliber machine-gun. Another round of fire barked, sounding more like a war up there than rival criminal gang factions.

"Is he going to be okay?" she asked. "Should we have stayed?"

"He's got the Devil's own luck. He'll be okay." His face firmed, though, as though he wished he had stayed to ensure his proclamation. After winding through the passages, he slowed as he approached a door. "You hear anything?" he whispered.

Sucking in a breath, she held it, opened her senses. Gunpowder wafted from behind them, but the gunshots had ended. Could be good or bad, depending on who won. "Other than what's behind us, I don't hear anything."

"We're on the opposite side of the building we parked next to. We might encounter some resistance. Also, it stands to reason the elf has been found and my father knows, and they've already come looking for us. Going back to the villa is dangerous. But, I think there's a good chance he attacked West, thinking he'd scoop me up too. If he's short funds, he can't afford full staffing of his vampire guards. He may have put the majority of his efforts here, leaving him under-protected. I think this may be our chance to confront him and bring him in. Your thoughts?"

Some information went on one side of the odds-calculation scale, some facts on the other. But in the end, she had only one answer. "You know him better than I do. If you think this is our chance, let's do it."

"The Clan Sanguis way is to fight to the death, so it may get dicey."

Her mouth dried. She'd never been more ready to fight next to someone. For Hetty. For him. A lump formed in her throat, one she had to swallow before she could say, "Born ready."

A dangerous, grim smile crossed his face, reminiscent of the great whites who made the San Francisco Bay home. "Dynamic to the SUV, okay? You good with running six?" His words said they'd move fast, him on point, with her responsibility being whatever threat came from behind.

"Got it," she said. "I'm going to take your belt loop."

He moved to the door and she hooked two fingers through the loop as promised. The connection would ensure he didn't leave her behind, since her eyes would be elsewhere and moving backward could be awkward. He threw open the door and stepped out, Lily on his heels, gun hand pointed in the direction they'd emerged, covering his back. They made it around the corner of the building and to the SUV without incident. Cal reversed the vehicle and exited the warehouse district from a different street.

She'd turned in her seat to monitor their rear, while Cal pushed the pedal to the floor. "I think I may know who is behind the conspiracy." He swerved into the left lane and passed a car. "In case I don't make it out and you do, give this information to Simon deVrys, my Deputy Director. If he's not available, to Alannah Johnson. No one else."

Her stomach clenched, and not from his driving. She sketched a glance to him. His hands gripped the wheel with surety, eyes laser-focused on the road. "We're going to make it out," she said, forcing confidence into her words.

He braked, switched lanes, accelerated again. "When I entered Tyron's mind, he told me he reported to a 'Zack.' The image associated was Clan Fae's Council Representative.

Whoa. "Does the Fae Queen know?"

He slowed at a fresh red light, made a right turn, then an immediate U-turn. Another right turn at the green light and he guided them back on the original path, minus attracting police attention for violating traffic laws. "If top-level fae leadership is involved, this goes all the way to her. Kalypso wouldn't stand for disobedience. And it fits her pattern. She used fear and intimidation, along with outright violence, to murder the prior king and his queen if whispers from the realm are to be believed."

Lily blew a light whistle. "Not all's happy-happy in the Fae Realm, then?"

"Not right now," he said, brows lowered. "And from what I've learned, Kalypso isn't the type to be satisfied with her own realm. She'll always look for more. More misery and more power. Simon will understand." The SUV's tires screeched as he made a corner, slowing a bit in the residential neighborhood.

"If you've got it figured out, why are we confronting your father?"

"If I'm right, I need him for testimony. His empire is close to crumbling. He'll go to ground soon. Also, he may have more information on conspirators than Kalypso." He parked at the trailhead where they'd emerged earlier. "It'll be faster," he said in response to her raised brows and the unspoken question of why they didn't park at his safe house.

He didn't take the same path, rather went up the canyon on the wide, well-worn route at a fast clip, but not enough to wind her. He cut right after several minutes.

As if sensing her question, he said, "Different way in. The place is riddled with them. Raum needs his escape routes, just like West." He came to a wall of boulders, but one slit was wide enough to shimmy through and into a passage.

Damp haunted her nose. Other than her and Cal, she couldn't pick up demon scents. It must've been a long time since anyone had been through. Lights, spaced far apart, offered the sparest amount of illumination for them to make their way. The steep grades and stairs left her sucking air as he navigated through a maze of tunnels.

Cal slowed, then stopped as the floor evened out. "We're close now." His voice dipped in volume.

"Plan?" She controlled her breathing through her nose.

"He'll be in his study, holed up, waiting for news from them. It's on the first floor. We're coming in on the sub-basement level."

"Can we use the secret passage we took to Grigori's rooms to get to the study?"

Cal shook his head. "He'll suspect them. I had hoped we would make it back before Raum returned." He put his free hand on her upper arm. "Hopefully he'll devote most of his remaining guards to watching the route we took earlier. This way puts us on the correct side of the villa, but we'll have to climb two sets of servant's stairs to the first floor, then make it to his study. I'd put the odds at fifty-fifty we make it to him without bloodshed."

She snorted. "That good, eh?"

A corner of his mouth rose, and his gaze softened a bit. "After this is done, I'm going to have to convince you to stick around."

It didn't sound exactly like he offered her a job, but more, a chance. With him. Her heart skipped. Not to let him think she was easy, she jammed her free hand on her hip and cocked her eyebrow. "I'd put the odds at fifty-fifty on that."

"Better odds than I thought." His grin glowed bright in the dim light.

"That's *if* we get out of here. Now let's go get your asshole father and make him cough up the four-one-one on this conspiracy. I've got your back."

His grin blinded her. "Okay...partner. Stay close."

A couple more turns resulted in a stone wall. He put his hand toward the corner and the wall pivoted easily from a central point. And most importantly, without a noise.

She followed Cal into a storeroom of some sort, filled with furniture and boxes.

Gun pointed forward, he led the way, while she continued watching their six. No one else in the sub-basement. He stopped midway up the first set of stairs and she halted immediately. He tucked his weapon in the small of his back, held up one finger, pointed ahead, then dragged it against his neck. *One guard, going to go cut his throat.*

She nodded her understanding.

From his pocket, he pulled a large folding knife, extended the blade, then squeezed her shoulder, the sign he was going to move.

She stayed with him until he reached the landing. Careful breaths went in her nose, then out her mouth, a technique to control the situation's stress but also get scents. Her heart hadn't kicked up to full battle mode yet, so she could still use her shifter-enhanced hearing to pick up approaching footfalls.

Cal lightly clicked his tongue once, a signal indicating he was returning. He appeared at her side, gun in hand, and resumed point. The metallic tang of fresh blood came with him in his wake. She stayed close until they reached the opening to the courtyard.

"His study is along this wall. Two doors." He barely breathed the words, but enough for her hearing to pick them up.

Fingers still wrapped in his belt loop, she pressed her knuckles against him in silent acknowledgement. *Nut cuttin' time.* She inhaled a deep breath, then pushed it out to settle any nerves wanting to get jumpy. Cal rounded the corner, Lily in tow.

A guard appeared around the corner they'd just rounded. "Gun," she said, squeezing the trigger four times, two to the heart, two to the head. She hadn't paused her backward steps, firing on the move.

The vampire dropped, but not before a bullet whizzed over her shoulder. She'd barely had time to start congratulating herself for the good shot when two more guards appeared. She squeezed off more rounds. Hebert Security team members were expected not to miss. She didn't, all three hit the ground. But not before she heard a swift intake of breath from Cal.

She bumped into him as he halted, frustration blossoming. Over her shoulder, twenty or so guards appeared in the second-floor gallery across the courtyard, another ten or more from around the corner, stepping over the ones she shot.

Dammit. Her gut churned. No wonder it'd been so easy. They'd walked into a trap.

"Put your weapons down." An authoritative voice said, one awfully similar to Cal's.

"Do it." Cal said.

Her teeth gritted, but she couldn't see any other option. With a curse, she placed the automatic on the smooth terrazzo. From the corner of her eye, Cal's ass appeared, so he obviously did the same, minus the audible swear word.

Tall, bulky vampire guards advanced, guns still sighted on her. She assumed the same happened in the other direction.

One of the vampires clamped a giant hand around her upper arm, yanked her forward, pushing her to the ground. He stripped the backpack from her, and as quickly, manacles snapped around her wrists. Ouch. The last one pinched skin. His foot stepped on her head, the rubber tread grinding her cheek into the smooth surface, while another pair of vampire's hands searched her body, lingering in places they shouldn't. Like her boobs, crotch, and butt.

She bit back a string of swear words with the questing hands. Not like she could open her jaw anyway. If she saw who did it, though... Retribution might hurt, but the cost would be worth it. She gritted her teeth as fingers closed over her nipple and squeezed. *And he'd be first.*

The giant vampire who'd been stepping on her yanked her to her feet. Another guard, this one with slicked-back dark hair, leered with a sick sneer.

She leaned forward and snarled, her wolf so close to the surface, it registered as an animal's.

He jumped back to the snickers of the dozen soldiers around them.

She'd have to wait for the right time to transform her hands and wrists into paw and leg. Unless enchanted, the bindings would slide off. But not yet. Raum still had too many soldiers. She needed to balance the scale. A plan began to form.

The slimy guard raised his hand to punch her.

Did he really think he could beat her reaction time? She almost laughed. As if.

His hand started forward, but Surgat stopped him.

"Not yet, idiot," the assistant hissed. His gaze slid to her, then did the up and down with a vile smile. "You'll have plenty of time later for games."

Rage exploded, so hot it almost blinded her. *Oh yeah. This fucker's gonna be toast too.*

Her captor spun her around and shoved her forward.

She stumbled, silently promising a round of much deserved ass-kicking to all three of them, as well as the demon standing ahead. Clothed in a severely-tailored black suit, with curly black hair cut in a fashionable mop, a tinge of olive-tan in his skin, cold black eyes with little hint of a pupil. All he'd need would be a scythe and he'd be the modern image of an arrogant young Death, barely out of his twenties. Yet, the resemblance was there. The shape of his jaw, the hairline on his forehead.

Lord Raum. Cal's father.

CHAPTER 16

If Cal had access to a brick wall, he'd beat his head against it. He should've sensed a trap. But he'd misjudged the strength of his father's forces. Instead, he'd kept them here, probably sending a smaller group to West's.

Dammit. He'd accept his fate if not for Lily. One thing if you got yourself killed due to sheer stupidity, a whole other discussion to get someone else killed. Or worse, drained to near death over and over until the night when one of them went too far. Like his mother's fate. Lily's blood may not nourish them, but that wouldn't stop the men from their sport.

Fury burned in his belly, making him want to roar. No. That would satisfy his father. Cal had to figure a way to get his mate to safety.

The guard marched him and Lily into the study, stopping him several paces from the front of Raum's desk. Surrounded by ancient tomes never read and art works gathered for their price, the piece of furniture had to be twice the size of any desk Cal had ever seen, a testament to his father's inadequacy issues. He'd bought this show palace, his title, all so he could be a big demon and treat everyone like shit. *What an asshole.*

Said asshole stalked past Cal to settle himself behind the wide expanse of desk. He didn't even spare a glance for his own son. Surgat paced in his master's shadow and placed himself behind and to the right of the seated lord.

Lily appeared in his peripheral vision. The soldier guiding her dumped the backpack at her feet. How they hadn't searched it yet showed the poor training and personnel his father employed. She'd stowed two guns earlier—there should be one left in the pack. Plus, the fae gold pen, which could be booby trapped. Hmm...

She shook off the demon's heavy paw. "Touch me again and I'll make you eat a dozen whale shifter dicks," she growled.

That's my Lily. That her fight was still there gave him hope.

"The shifter will be silent," his father ordered.

Lily's head snapped forward, eyes narrowed. Somehow she remained quiet. Silently plotting his disembowelment, no doubt.

He could plead to the man's sanity. For Lily's sake. "Father. You should let her go. She's a NACS agent. Harming her will do you no good now."

Raum turned his gaze to Cal and raked him up and down with a sneer. "And you will be silent as well. You are not my son and know the penalty for calling me your sire in public."

Oh yes, he remembered. And it would make watching his father's downfall all that sweeter. As long as he could get them out of this situation. Subtle vibrations gently buffeted him. What...?

Lily. She'd quieted alright, to the point where her snarl stayed below audible range.

His heart lightened a little at her support. A plan started to form. "I think you want to hear what I have to say, *Father.*" Despite Lord Raum's stiffening in his chair, Cal plowed on. "But I don't think you want to hear it in front of these vampires." He couldn't gesture to Surgat or the eight guards in the room with his hands, since they were bound behind his back.

Information. Currency sometimes worth more than a fortune. And as the NACS Director, he would have access to a lot of information. Something in Cal's voice must've made an impact. His father paled, but his upper lip rose even more. "What makes you think I want to hear anything you have to say?"

"Because it may mean the difference between mere disgrace and imprisonment. Maybe even death, once NAC Courts are done with you. If they can get to you before the King." He stuffed as much contempt into his words as would fit.

The older demon jumped to his feet, face blood-reddened. "Get out." His words dropped like bombs in the room and the vampire guards hastened to comply. "Not you, Surgat, or you." He pointed at the big guard next to Lily.

The slightest hint of satisfaction crossed the guard's face, as if happy to be selected while all the others were banished.

Poor, stupid vampire. After what Cal had to say, his father would most likely kill the big lunk. Cal found little compassion. His father hired mercenaries and criminals, mostly rogue vampires, though he hid it from the King. The worst of the most evil Clan Sanguis had to offer. It would probably be some justice for whatever the vampire had done but for which he hadn't received retribution.

The door snapped shut, leaving Surgat and the guard as his father's only protectors. Much better odds.

"What is it you wanted to tell me that's so important?" Lord Raum crossed his arms.

The bored tone didn't fool Cal. If West's information proved correct, hiring those thugs may have cost him his last of his bloody fortune. "Very well." No sugar coating here. Only acid. "Grigori is dead. The *real* Grigori."

For a moment, utter stillness, not even a blink or a breath, was his father's reaction. Then he sat abruptly, as if his legs wouldn't hold him any longer.

"And the best part, *Father*, is the NAC knows you let him out." No quarter. His father had never given any. "And they'll know shortly how you've been funding the conspiracy to help take over the Council."

"They promised—" His father cut off the admission, his nostrils flaring. "You don't know he's dead."

By not denying his complicity in the conspiracy, his father as good as admitted to it. So satisfying. That meant he worried more about Grigori, his precious heir, than going to jail or being sentenced to death. Which then lead to the confirmation the great Lord Raum was probably in the red, and it made Cal's next words all the sweeter.

"He's dead alright. Blew up in NACS morgue yesterday. You can choose to believe me or not, but this agent was with me and witnessed the explosion as well. It's best if you come clean. Tell me who your coconspirators were. King Krian and his Court will disavow you—they will honor their pact with the HP over you. You'll find no support there." Time to bait the hook. "And Kalypso won't help you either."

Raum's Adam's apple bobbed. "If the body was blown up, then you have no proof it was him." A blood-alcoholic sucking the meager drops from his last bottle sounded less desperate. And less in denial. And again, no contradiction of Cal's Kalypso reference.

Bingo.

"You are seriously not going to believe him?" Lily cocked her head to the side, a contemptuous half-smile on her face. "Your own son. The one you're petitioning the King to acknowledge?"

"He's not my *legitimate* son. He's nothing but a bastard." He'd regained his mantle of imperious authority. He turned to Surgat. "Take them to the dungeons and make sure you get every scrap of information from them. Then kill the bastard. You can give the female to the vampires."

Gods dammit. She would not end up like his mother.

"For the love of the Great Wolf. Your precious sociopath son and heir is dead. As in, no longer breathing. We put him to bed with a shovel. You know. He's taking a dirt nap." She chuckled with her crude euphemisms. And Cal loved her for it, though he couldn't fathom her intention to anger Raum further.

"Silence," the demon bellowed, his color shooting beyond red straight to purple.

While the shade appeared apoplectic, demons wouldn't have heart attacks or strokes. Making him more irate would only result in worse torture. "Lily, he's not going to believe you. Doesn't matter."

She slid him a hard glance that said *back off*.

What was the little vixen up to?

With a half step forward, she leaned toward Lord Raum. "I don't give a shit if he believes me or not, it matters. Because *I* smelled the shithead's stinking, rotting corpse. After they removed his brain, there was nothing left but a green-yellow slimy mess. They took his ears, his nose. But left his dick and balls behind." She husked a laugh. "Then dressed him up like an HP and tacked him to the wall of a shed in Split, Texas to decompose. I wonder how he fucked up to deserve that end? Your perfect son was murdered by the very people you're supporting. And it makes me laugh at how pathetic you are. Thinking Kalypso would make you part of her new empire. What a moron."

Cal had kept his gaze trained on his father, to catch the subtle nuances of his expression as she informed him of his son's demise, the smothered horror, the pain. But now her voice had become forced, like she talked through agony, and Cal turned to her, expecting the guard to have grabbed her.

She swayed, then recovered, jaw firming, her breathing labored. "And now, you're about to lose your entire empire, your businesses, your reputation, your fucking castle, your...freedom.

I...feel...so...not...sorry...for...you. Asshole." Her last word came on a whisper.

No one caught her as she crumpled to the thick carpet. She curled on herself, writhing on the floor.

Cal's heart hit his ribcage hard, then started pumping triple-time as he dropped to his knees. "What's wrong? Lily? Lily?" He worked his wrists against the restraints. What happened to her? He jumped to his feet and took a step toward the desk before the huge vampire guard pulled him back. "What did you do to her?"

His father had recovered by then and laughed, the cruelty in the sound would've made Ivan the Terrible proud. "She's a weak shifter. Who knows what happened to her, much less cares?"

"You'll care. If I'm not back at NAC, all the information I have goes directly to Council Chair Johnston."

Lord Raum waived a dismissive hand, confidence rallied. "When—if—they come looking for you, you will have gone to visit that Westryn Roark scum you liked to hang out with. I can't help it if you associated with a terrible crowd and died.

The doors burst open. "*We* can certainly help that. Hands up."

Cal spun at Berith's welcome voice.

Officers Sand and Maximino Espina stood in front of the doors forming a wide, loose triangle with the Captain. He blinked. Why were they here?

Lily's weak chuckle rose from the floor. How did she know...

A spell flashed overhead and Cal dove to cover her body.

For several moments, he protected her from any of the crashes or explosions during the fight. His most talented officers could handle his father and remaining vampires. When her lids fluttered shut, he said, "Hang on, Lily. We'll get you help soon."

The commotion died down and Cal lifted his head to find Sand standing over him. A wave of her fingers caused his bindings to fall away. He scrambled to his knees and put his hand on Lily's shoulder. She wouldn't waken. His heart froze. No. It couldn't be.

He put his finger under her nose, shallow wafts of air blew by. Still breathing. Relief swamped him. "We have to get her to the med ward."

"Boss, we'll get her there shortly. She'll be fine," Sand said as she laid a hand on his shoulder, admiration glowing in her eyes. "She's violated the secrecy provision of her contract. That's why we're here. Pretty damn smart female."

Violated the secrecy provision? He rocked back on his heels, stunned. He'd never thought to use the rule that way. Probably because he wasn't party to the same proviso, but damn. The spell carved a chunk from her life to teleport the security personnel here, and Lily's body didn't agree with the taking. He took in his little shifter, light freckles standing out against her pale skin. He brushed away a tendril of mahogany hair from her cheek. She was something. And his. He would make sure she stayed around. He merely had to find the right incentive.

"We're ready, sir," Berith said. He had control of Lord Raum, his hands bound behind his back, a tear in the shoulder of his costly suit jacket. His mouth had slackened and eyes grown distant as he stood there, defeat written in the slump of his shoulders. Despite Cal's overwhelming sense of victory, it came with a sense of pity for the demon.

Why?

Grigori's death would never have made his father turn to Cal with sudden acceptance. Certainly wouldn't offer him any apologies for treating him worse than a blood slave all those years.

Indeed, he is to be pitied. He missed out on a wonderful son. His mother's gentle laugh echoed in his head.

Yes. Cal would pity him. In pursuit of power and wealth, all Raum's drive had been wasted.

Except that portion he gave to Cal. Lily had been correct in that respect.

Movement pulled him from his thoughts. Espina led a limping

Surgat by, hands also bound. The NACS officer jerked his chin in acknowledgement, which Cal returned. That officer, once an assassin, was quickly becoming a star in the ranks. It wouldn't be long until he promoted to sergeant or went into the investigative side as an agent.

The guard lay feet away, bound, suffering from Espina's magical scorpion's sting. Either way, the vampire would be interrogated, on the off-chance they could drag useful information from him. Officer Sand levitated the vampire and trailed her compatriots from the room.

Time to go. He picked up Lily's bag and slung it over his shoulder. Then he put his hands under her knees and shoulders, careful to jar her as little as possible. She frowned, writhed a bit, but for the most part, the extreme pain had knocked her out.

He exited the study behind his officers and passed the fountain, with its carved marble figures of Cupid and Psyche.

He needed to figure out how to keep Lily with him. A plan started to form.

CHAPTER 17

Two days after she'd experienced the worst pain her little pea-canine brain could imagine, Chip stomped down the hallway to the Director's office when she should've been on her way to a sunny beach and margaritas. Someone had fucked up her contract payment.

Nobody messed with her money.

She fiddled with the leather-tabbed zipper on her motorcycle jacket with agitated fingers. At least someone returned her belongings from the villa. She hugged the familiar hide to her. Hetty had given it to her and she'd have hated to lose it after so much time. And now Chip Foster was back in all her ass-kicking, smart-mouthed glory.

Thankful the spell had done its job, then been counteracted by the doctors, she pulled in a deep breath. It had clamped on all of her muscles—heart and lungs included—with such ferocity, she couldn't believe she still lived. Great idea for a rescue, but maybe someone else could do it next time.

Abraham ceased his tapping on the computer and looked up over half glasses with limpid gray eyes, which matched his hair.

The HP's tone complemented his expression—devoid of emotion. "He's waiting for you."

"Thank you." Lily wanted to march on by without comment, but Aunt Hetty drilled manners into her long ago, despite the feral cub wanting nothing to do with the stupid useless things. She kept the rage rolling underneath, though. All the better to ignore her wolf, the one in the back of her mind howling Cal's name.

Back off. He's not your mate. And that's Director Stavros remember? She huffed an impatient breath. You know I have to track. I can't work here as his subordinate and still be with him. At least according to Mr. By-the-Book. You know what Lone Wolf means and you accepted that fact long ago. Gah. The whining is driving me nuts. We're going back to the bayou and Hebert Security.

Her wolf went back to her howls, this time of *No*.

Damn dog. She didn't bother to knock on the thick panel, instead, threw it open with a little more force than needed. It bounced back, but she caught the careening heavy door before it hit her in the nose.

A male sat in front of the Director's desk. He turned and rose as she entered, thick gorgeous chestnut hair, a model's chiseled features, sparkling whiskey eyes, and emitting the HP scent. The lean-muscled body in the close-cut suit would make most women swoon.

Yet, for all his perfection, he paled before the demon behind the desk. Even in a black polo and cargo pants, both which molded to his physique to perfection, he drew her eyes like a dang feral dog to a three-day old carcass.

Hungry.

Cal—Director Stavros—rose to his feet upon her entry. A business smile for welcome, no more. Mr. By-the-Book definitely made his return. She'd made the right choice to leave the Rock, especially since she hadn't seen him since she woke yesterday evening in the med ward.

At least the prior three days weren't for naught. Last night he'd told her of his father's confession. Combined with West's financial information and the remaining evidence, he'd turned the case over to Constantine for legal to figure out how to handle. Taking action against a council representative couldn't be taken lightly. Cal said he had a detail monitoring the fae party's movements until a decision was made. The careful, neutral tone he'd used to inquire about her health and make his report confirmed she'd made the right decision to leave. He regretted kissing her, driving her wild with need.

"Foster. Thank you for coming," Cal—Director Stavros, dammit—said.

Her mouth dried and she swallowed. What had she expected, him to sweep her off her feet? Swear his undying love? By her faithless ancestors, she must get her money and leave before she did something she regretted. Like leap at him and tear his clothing off with her teeth. "Thank you for coming? I was told I had to come see you because somebody screwed up my check. If you can get it cut, I'll be on my way."

"I don't know why they'd send you up here. Have a seat here while I make a call. This is Grant Knotts. Grant, this is Lil...Chip Foster." He picked up his phone's handset and pushed some buttons. Since Cal started speaking, someone must have answered.

Where had she heard Grant Knotts's name before? It tickled the back of her brain, but the damn wolf's howling made her teeth ache, and for sure wouldn't allow her gray matter function properly.

"Chip Foster, eh? I've heard a lot about Clan Shifter's best tracker."

She took his outstretched hand. During the handshake, which went on a bit too long, his gaze darted around her. She disengaged, wary of this male, and plopped into the plush leather chair. "You can't inspect my teeth."

Knotts resumed his seat as well with a hitch to his pantlegs and laughed. "I'd also heard you had a good sense of humor. I think you and Cal are perfect for each other."

Her heart stopped, then thumped wildly. She took a second to recover. "Wha-what gave you the idea we'd be good together? I mean, it's not like we're mates or anything. Until he gets this damn paperwork straightened out, he's my boss."

She couldn't suppress the wince as the howls intensified with the lies and excuses tumbling from her lips. *Girl, you better shut it.*

"I guess you haven't heard of me, then." Knotts pulled a card from his pocket and presented it to her.

In a bold, masculine script the small rectangle simply read *Grant Knotts. The Mate-Maker.* A telephone number and email landed in the lower right corner.

The glossy card with its simple lettering almost slipped from her shaking fingers as the name and the business finally connected. *What the fuck?* She handed it back to him. "You've got the wrong female."

He accepted it gracefully and slid it back into his pocket. "I'd also heard you were stubborn."

"I'm not—"

"Another good quality to have, because so is Cal. You won't let him ride roughshod over you. And he's too serious. You'll keep him on his toes." His model smile returned, all perfect white teeth. "Your auras align like few I've seen."

Shit. Shit. *Come on Chip, do your damn job.* "You need to put those teeth to use in a toothpaste ad, because you're obviously no good at matches." He laughed aloud this time, as if she hadn't insulted him. She couldn't detect any frustration or anger pheromones, either. A growl formed in her throat.

"I know my business, those who, no matter the protestations of love, won't make it. And those who, despite objections otherwise, are perfect for each other." He turned to Cal, who wasn't on the phone any longer, just sitting back, watching their exchange.

Anger rose in a wave to swamp her.

"*You* brought him here. And paid him to say this to me. What is this? A joke?" Her voice had risen. When had she jumped to her feet? "Is this some sort of sick joke?"

She tried to get ahold of her breathing and her heart, which had squeezed painfully before slamming in her ribcage. Great. Now she repeated herself. She scouted an escape route, the only one known was the door she'd entered.

"Thanks for coming, Grant. We'll talk soon," Cal said.

"No worries, my friend." The Mate Maker's lips twisted. "For what it's worth, I think you're going to have your hands full trying to convince her. Good luck."

She tracked him as he left the office. "What in the hell was that, Ca—Director Stavros?"

"That was my apparently very poor plan to try to convince you you're my mate. And I'm yours." He didn't make excuses. Didn't apologize. As if he'd accepted the fact and knew she'd fight it.

Listen to him. Make you happy.

Shut up! She slammed the door on her wolf.

"Poor plan? It was the sorriest possible way to try to get me to believe we're mates." She crossed her arms. "What are you going to do next? Pull my braid?"

He rose and rounded the desk, determination etched in every line of his features. "If I have to." He stopped in front of her.

No backing down. Keep that underbelly safe. Rather than budging, she craned her neck with her best Chip Foster glare while trying to rein in her panicked breathing and heart. She licked her dry lips, then said, "I'd like to see you try."

"I don't want to try. I'd rather do this." His head lowered.

Not fast enough that she couldn't have evaded him. She stood there, frozen, wanting the touch of his lips with the entirety of her being. But she'd been so convinced love would never be for her. And then his lips touched hers, soft, asking, allowing her to decide if she'd pull away. Cindering all doubts. She threw her arms around his neck and pulled him closer. Not enough. She jumped, wrapped her legs around his hips.

He deepened the kiss, his velvet tongue stroking, lips slanting, a mating dance. He turned and sat her on the desk where her legs cradled him, already hard and thick and ready for her.

Need skittered along her skin. Contact. She must touch him. Lick him. Everywhere. Do everything to him. Now. One of her hands moved from clutching his hair and slid down his hard chest. His muscles contracted as she dragging her nails down, across his hard pectorals, his abs, and lower, to where his cock pulsed against her hand.

Her wolf's sighs of pleasure matched Lily's.

A harsh buzz from behind her made her pull back. "Director, Council Chair Johnston is here to see you," Abraham announced through the speaker.

Great Wolf, the NAC Council Chair? Lily pushed against his chest to release her, but he wouldn't budge.

Cal rumbled a laugh. "Tell her I'll be with her in a minute."

"Uh, ma'am...Okay, here."

"You and Foster stay right there." Alannah Johnston's voice came over the speaker. "Come see me when you're done with your shifter, Director Stavros." The click indicated the intercom had disconnected.

Lily's cheeks heated. A strong clairvoyant, the Council Chair had obviously picked up on the activity on the other side of the door.

"She has impeccable timing." He shoved a hand through his hair, a charming, rueful smile crossing his face. His hand dropped to cradle her cheek. "But I'm not done with you. I don't know that I'll ever be done with you, Moonlight Lily Foster."

But demons needed the blood to contact fully with their mate. "What about biting me?"

"If I have to, I'll bite the pillow." His mouth twisted. "Blood's important, but not the end all. I want you, even if I can't have your delicious, intoxicating blood."

Delicious? Intoxicating? Her face grew warm and she studied the top button of his polo for a moment before she lifted her deep gold gaze to his. "I have a confession. When we kissed, I wouldn't have minded if you took a little sip. I know I'm safe with you."

"Oh Gods." The words emerged a bit strangled. He swooped down, taking her lips in another fiery kiss.

Several moments later, she disengaged. "The kissing is all well and fine, but how are we going to make this work?" she said through her heavy breaths. "I'm not going to give up tracking and Director By-the-Book can't be my boss."

"That's where I have a plan." He waggled his eyebrows.

"A plan?"

He nodded slowly, solemnly. "A plan. You won't work for me. You work for Hebert Security. On contract, as needed. But you come home to me. Always come home to me."

The words sank into her mind, into her soul. Her wolf howled, a cry of joy this time. She folded her hands against his chest and nodded. "I promise. As long as you do the same. You're not some pencil-necked paper-pusher either."

He fit his forehead against hers. "Deal. I had no idea the smart-mouthed, authority-defying female who kneed me in the balls four days ago would end up being the mate I needed."

"And I never realized the stuffed-shirt, stick-up-his-ass male who quoted regulations to me all the time would end up being the mate I needed." She tipped her head, set her lips to his.

Alannah would have to wait a while. This wolf shifter wouldn't be done with her demon for some time.

A Note from Amanda Reid

Hello! Just a short message to say I hope you enjoyed this book and to ask if you would leave a review of *The Deomon's Shifter Mate*? We independently published authors need your input, as do other readers to find the stories they want to read. It can be as simple or as detailed as you like. And thank you in advance!

Also, check out my website for an awesome *FREE* novella, *The Puma's Second Chance*, available when you sign up for my newsletter, which will also feature promos, insights into my little writing world (its okay—y'all know me here!), and other awesome stuff. Check out www.amandareidauthor.com for more details.

Until we read again,
Amanda

PS—Turn the page for my next exciting Enchanted Rock Immortals novella, T*he Fae's Obsession*!

The Fae's Obsession
An Enchanted Rock Immortals Novella
by Amanda Reid

Obsession...

Elf Simon deVrys is assigned his toughest investigation yet, one which could bring down the entire North American Council. Now if he could only pull his thoughts from Talia, the beautiful, snarky woman who's stolen his heart, he could concentrate on locating the impossible, someone who can gain testimony from the dead. Never in his wildest, hottest dreams does he imagine the object of his obsession holds the key to obtaining the information he needs and to freeing his family from a decades-old threat.

Talia Johnson might've left her boring job as NAC Security's receptionist months ago, since getting yelled at on the daily by obnoxious clan elites sucked. But if she quit, how would she get her regular dose of the scrumptious elf Deputy Director? Obsessed with the gorgeous, fierce fae, Talia holds her own dangerous psychic secret, one other paranormals will kill to obtain.

Can Simon and Talia weather threats from those they should trust the most to find a love beyond mere obsession?

***The Fae's Obsession* is available in paperback, Kindle and Kindle Unlimited!**

ACKNOWLEDGMENTS

There are so many people to acknowledge in an author's life. First is family. Without my mother's love of reading, I may not be an author today. The same could be said about my father's determination, because any author will tell you, if you don't have drive, you will not make it past the first manuscript draft.

I certainly couldn't do this without my husband, who supports me in this effort every single day. Without that support, I wouldn't be releasing my fifth book, with three more yet to publish in 2020.

And again, my sisters in writing, the Enchanted Rock Immortals authors, Eve, Fenley, Robyn, and Susan. Their encouragement and teamwork made this effort possible.

Finally, my editor, Dawn Alexander with Dawn Alexander Books, and the Enchanted Rock cover artist, J. Kathleen Cheney. Each brings their excellent specialties to make these novellas sparkle.

Thank you to all. I am humbled by your support!

ABOUT THE AUTHOR

Amanda Reid is an author in the Enchanted Rock Immortals world of urban fantasy romance novellas. She also authors The Flannigan Sisters Psychic Mysteries, a series of light paranormal cozy mystery novellas.

Since she was young, she's been a lover of mystery, sci-fi, and paranormal books. Amanda found her first romance book in her aunt's closet around thirteen years of age and quickly decided it needed to be added to her repertoire. As do many readers, she'd always dreamed of writing. She finally learned the secret, and she'll let you in on it--do it. That simple and that hard.

Beyond writing, Amanda was a career Army brat and lived in exotic locations like Tehran, Iran and DeRidder, Louisiana as a child. She obtained an International Politics degree and dreamed of a career in the State Department, but ended up as a federal agent. Amanda spent 24 years investigating murders, fraud, identity theft, drug trafficking and many other crimes before her retirement. As you can imagine, it's given her a wealth of inspiration for her mystery and urban fantasy stories.

She currently lives in Texas with her husband and two gonzo Australian Shepherds. Catch up with her on Twitter or Facebook. You can sign up for upcoming releases and promos at amandareidauthor.com.

Enchanted
Rock
Immortals

Made in the USA
Columbia, SC
13 November 2024